Night and Day

Dinah Barber

Contents

Chapter 1

Alistair Stevens took a deep, steadying breath and asked for guidance before he stepped out to join his Aunt Lizzy on the terrace of their Texas ranch house. Lizzy stared vacantly at the beautiful view of the valley before them, and Alistair was at a loss as to how he could help her.

He placed his arm around her shoulders and pulled her close as she turned into him with a sniffle.

"I can't believe he is gone. I can't believe I will never get to see his face or feel his arms around me again," Lizzy choked on a sob that racked her body.

They had just buried her husband, Brian Alexander, that morning. He had been taken so quickly that it was hard for any of them to believe he was gone. To the family, it felt as if he was only in the next room or away on one of his many business trips, but Lizzy felt his loss in her soul. She knew he was gone and appeared to have aged overnight because of it.

Alistair rested his head on hers as he squeezed her shoulders. "I'm sorry you're so sad, and I'm sure Brian would be too," Alistair whispered.

"I am sad, but I am also mad!" Lizzy shook her head. "Your Uncle Brian wasted eight years of our lives that we could have been together. I never resented that time we lost until now. Now that he's gone, I keep thinking we could have had eight more years together. Eight more years of memories, but his stubborn ass had to listen to your father!"

"My father?" Alistair asked.

"Yes, I was twenty and in love with Brian, who was thirty-three, and your father, my brother, thought that I was too young, so he told Brian to back off, and he did. It took us eight years to reunite." Lizzy exhaled, and her shoulders were heavy in her sorrow.

"What brought you back together?" He was confused at the idea that his father could have caused so much havoc. Generally, Bryce Stevens was a live-and-let-live kind of fellow. He even kept well out of Alistair's life, letting him live it the way he wanted, so long as Alistair understood the title would one day be his and he would have to accept the responsibility when the time came.

"The same thing that drove us apart, your father. He fell in love with your mother, realized what he had done, and fixed it." Lizzy's voice softened. "So, Bryce is why I lost him and found him again, but I wish to God that Brian would have told your father to go hang himself and swept me away from it all." Lizzy swallowed hard. "If he had, we could have had eight more years together."

"Do you think the heartache of being apart made it that much sweeter when you were finally together?" Alistair thought about his life and the choices he had made or had not made. "Perhaps, knowing what it was like when you couldn't have him made it mean so much more when you did, and that made your relationship stronger than it would have been otherwise?"

Lizzy turned and looked up at him, tilting her head as she absorbed her words.

"You sound like your mother, always looking for the bright side."

Alistair smiled at the compliment.

"You also sound like you know what you're talking about." When Alistair opened his mouth to object, Lizzy held up her hand to stop him from whatever he was about to say. "That's your business, but I will say that if you fall in love, really in love, move heaven and earth to be together because a day like today will come." Lizzy took a deep fortifying breath. "And as painful as it is, the only thing worse would be if that day didn't come because you never got to spend your life with the person you loved."

Alistair gave a forced smile, and a heavy silence descended on them for a moment as he did his best to keep all thoughts of Katherine Randolph at bay.

"Did you know that when your mother and I first met, I didn't like her? I thought she was after your father for his money. I think I was as determined to save him from her as he was to save me from Brian." Lizzy looked back at the view in front of her as her mind wandered into the past.

"I hear a but in there?" Alistair teased.

"But... your father truly thought he was protecting me, and I, sensing that something serious was happening because of family gossip, only wanted to hurt him. I wanted to hurt him the way he had hurt me, and I didn't care if it hurt your mother in the process." She let out a shaky sigh as if it was a relief to admit it.

"I've heard the story. Is that why you were all right with Rainer and my mother being a possible love match?" Alistair softly asked.

"Must have been," Lizzy agreed.

"What about Aunt Laura? You two still don't get along to this day. Surely, she has proven after thirty years that she's in it for the long haul?" Alistair joked.

"I honestly was trying to protect your Uncle Davis, and once that line was drawn, we were both too stubborn to erase it." Lizzy shrugged. "We are both too much alike to ever really get along anyway, but I believe we respect each other and would have the other's back if it came down to it."

"Family." Alistair nodded.

"Yes, for better or worse, your father and mother, myself and Laura, we are all family."

"Can I ask you a question? It's personal?" Alistair asked as he turned away from the view and looked down at Lizzy. "Why didn't you and Uncle Brian have any children?"

Lizzy shrugged. "We didn't want to share each other, we liked to travel, and with you and your cousins, it was never something we missed. Your Uncle also had a difficult childhood, and he didn't want to risk raising children and passing on bad traits to them."

"Uncle Brian was awesome with all of us when we were kids!" Alistair objected to the idea that Brian would have been anything but a great father.

Lizzy smiled at his outburst. "It's a case of nature and not nurture."

"The kids would have inherited the Stevens genes, I'm sure," Alistair insisted.

"Perhaps, but we'll never know. What about you? Do you want children one day?" It was a probing question. Sadness couldn't keep Aunt Lizzy down for long, and even though she had insisted that it was his business, she was still curious. He had learned the signs of a prying aunt when he was a kid.

"I don't really have a choice, do I?" He lifted an eyebrow in question.

"Sure you do. I'm sure there's a male cousin somewhere willing to take over the reins, but even if there's not, it's not the end of the world if the title dies out. Your father is not as attached to it as our father and grandfather were."

"It's a comforting thought," Alistair responded without really answering the question.

Of course, he would like children someday, an entire house full, but he would need a woman first, and the only woman he wanted had made it clear that she wasn't interested in anything permanent.

"You know what else is a comforting thought?" Alistair said as he gently turned his aunt toward the house. "Food and family. I hear Dad on the piano limbering up the keys, which means Aunt Cassie is about to sing something."

He led Lizzy into the warmth of the house, and as they entered, Poppy, the youngest cousin at 23, flew up to her holding out a magazine. "Aunt Lizzy, look what I found in Uncle Quinn's office!"

Lizzy took the magazine and dreamily sighed as she looked at the cover.

"That's Uncle Brian, isn't it?" Poppy asked.

"Yes, it was an interview that Uncle Rainer begged him to give, and your Uncle Davis took the photos." Lizzy opened the magazine to the four-page story on Brian. The photos showed him in different poses during the interview. He had started with his suit jacket on and a serious face, but by the end, he was sitting with his sleeves rolled up, tie askew, and a drink in his hand.

"He was dreamy!" Poppy said, looking over her aunt's shoulder.

"He was, and he was mine." Lizzy looked at Quinn, who was sitting on the sofa with Dana. "Can I keep this? I seem to have lost mine along the way." Her smile was shaky.

"Please." Quinn nodded.

Poppy and Lizzy sat at the large kitchen table and bent their heads together as they talked about the story. Poppy was interested in all things Stevens and the many stories her aunts and uncles chose to share. Evidently, she would become the family's archivist for future generations. They had thought it would be their cousin Beth many years ago, but then she fell in love and had a family then her interests changed.

Alistair looked over at Beth, who was tending to one of her children. He wanted to ask her how Katherine was doing since he knew they were close friends, but he didn't dare. He knew she would see right through him in an instant.

Perhaps it was time to try and woo the lady again. It had been a few years. Maybe circumstances had changed.

Chapter 2

K atherine set her phone on her lap and leaned her head against the back of her car seat as she watched the high-rises of New York fly by her window. She was on her way to the theater for a benefit concert. She had attended them many times but had never been part of one before.

It was a well-known Stevens family event, which meant the likelihood that she would see Alistair Stevens was strong. She hadn't seen him in over a year. Katherine couldn't suppress the little shiver that chased up her spine as she remembered their last meeting.

Their meetings were always intense and short. Whether it was a few nights in New York, London, or Paris, their nights together were always chance meetings and never planned. They ran in similar circles, so they met a few times every year. And every time they met, Katherine was determined to be strong and walk away, but it was an impossibility once she was near him.

Alistair was the only man who could make her melt with a look, and she was still confused about why he always chose her over so many other beautiful women. Their first meeting had been at a family birthday party eight years earlier. Katherine had seen him enter the party and had lost her heart then and there, but she had never lost her head.

At the time, she had just started her career, and she wasn't ready to settle into a relationship that might make her dependent on any man. Her mother had always been dependent on her father, and in making herself dependent, she had made all her daughters dependent. It had been a difficult road to escape, and Katherine didn't want to go back.

The phone in Katherine's lap vibrated again, and she looked at the message.

She would have to put her career on hold and go home. Her mother was sick, and her father asked her to come and nurse her. Katherine knew it was a ploy to force her back into the fold, but it was her mother. Her mother had done everything for her, protected her, and helped her escape when the time came. She couldn't abandon her now.

Katherine also knew her time at the top of runway modeling was almost over. At thirty-three, her career had lasted longer than most, and there was a strong chance that she would get to revive her television hosting gig in London after her leave of absence, but it wasn't guaranteed. She was no fool, and she realized that she was easily replaceable.

Her look was unique but not beautiful. In fact, she had believed that she was odd looking until Alistair's cousin, Beth, had told her she could model. It had offered her the escape she needed, and she had been independent for the last nine years.

The car stopped in front of the theater side entrance, and Katherine took a deep breath while waiting for the driver to come around and open her door. She reached for her dress and cosmetic case, then threw her long legs out of the car as she rose gracefully to her height of six feet.

She thanked the driver and ignored the flashbulbs as she entered the theater's busy backstage corridors while her phone vibrated in her pocket again. Ignoring it, she slowly walked down the long hall looking for the dressing room door that would have her name on it.

When Katherine found it, she took a steadying breath. She was sharing with Mave and Cassandra Stevens. Talk about leaping from the fire and into the frying pan. Cassandra was Alistair's aunt, and Mave was his cousin and Beth's fraternal twin.

The Stevenses were always kind to her, and if any of them suspected what was between her and Alistair, none of them showed it, not even her good friend, Beth.

Taking a moment to collect her thoughts and compartmentalize her personal issues, she put on her professional persona and opened the door with a genuine smile.

"Ladies," she greeted in her soft, pleasant voice.

"Katherine!" Beth greeted as she stood from the couch in the room to hug her. "I haven't seen you in over a year!"

"Has it been that long?" Katherine laughed as she hugged her back. "I can't believe it. I guess what they say about time speeding up as you get older is true."

"I can promise you it does," Cassandra assured her from where she sat in front of one of the dressing tables putting on lipstick.

She was still a beautiful woman. Her vibrant red hair had faded, but her skin was as lovely and unlined as it always had been, and her brown eyes were soft and welcoming.

"How are you, Mave?" Katherine asked as she took the table on the end, which placed Mave between her and Cassandra.

Mave gave one of her signature grins. "I'm great, Katherine, and yourself?"

"I'm well, thanks for asking," Katherine replied as she hung her dress on the peg attached to the side of the mirror and opened her makeup case.

Mave was always pleasant, but Katherine didn't feel she knew her well. She felt it was hard for anyone to really know Mave Stevens because her entire life was an act. However, Katherine couldn't judge her for it because her entire life was also an act.

"How's Wyatt and the girls?" Katherine asked Beth as she started to unpack her case.

"They're fine. Wyatt stayed home with them so I could come and keep you all company." Beth watched the women as they applied their stage makeup.

Katherine's mother and Wyatt Ramsey's stepmother had hoped that she and Wyatt would one day marry. Her mother had always been fond of Wyatt and knew he would care for her, and it would have been a way to get Katherine from under her father's thumb. However, Katherine and Wyatt had never felt anything close to romance. They got along well, and it was easy for them to attend events together, but it had never been more than that.

When Beth burst onto the scene, Katherine had watched her and Wyatt fall for each other and felt a little jealous, wanting to feel something similar. Then she met Alistair and felt the same kind of love, realizing it scared her to death.

While it took Beth and Wyatt a year to figure it out and get past the fear Wyatt felt, Katherine seemed unable to do the same where Alistair was concerned. Alistair had told her he loved her, but if he felt fear, he hid it well. She knew she was hurting Alistair and didn't want to, but if she gave him what he wanted to keep from hurting him, she knew it would only hurt him more in the long run.

"So, how was Paris?" Mave asked.

Katherine had just finished her runway shows for one of Paris's fashion weeks, and it had been bittersweet because she knew it was a strong chance that it was her last one. Katherine had never taken to photographic modeling. She had tried it earlier in her career, but she hated how she looked, so she preferred the runway. She wore clothes well, and the constant movement was better for her nerves.

"Paris was lovely." Katherine smiled. "I was surprised I didn't see any Stevens there."

The women were silent, and the vibe in the room changed from relaxed and friendly to overwhelmingly sad.

Katherine looked over her shoulder at Beth.

"We lost Uncle Brian a few weeks ago. It was sudden, an embolism." Beth gave a sad smile as she did her best to push back tears.

Katherine felt herself tear up as well. She had only met him a few times at parties, but she knew how much he meant to them all.

"I'm so very sad to hear that. How is Lizzy doing?" Katherine asked, thinking of the woman who always seemed to be meddling in someone's business, according to Beth.

"She's in Texas at the ranch taking it one day at a time." Mave blotted her lips and smiled in the mirror. "How do I look?" She stood up, twirling in her lovely baby blue dress that matched her eyes perfectly.

"Lovely as usual," Cassandra smiled.

"I'm guessing Cassandra is singing, and I know I'm hosting, but what role were you given, Mave?" Katherine asked as she started on her eye makeup.

"I'm narrating a mime." Mave gave a cheeky smile.

"Who's the mime?" Katherine asked.

Mave named an actor she supposedly dated until he got caught cheating on her. It had been all over the papers six months previously.

"Yes, the poor man didn't realize he would be teamed up with Mave until he arrived this evening." Beth was doing her best to hide her supportive grin.

"Mmm, yes, Mason was always good at helping you girls get even with those that dared to cross you. It's probably because he's such a girl himself." Cassandra sat back and looked at her handiwork.

"Did he tell you my part is unscripted?" Mave leaned into the mirror and tweaked her hair.

Katherine looked at Beth, who was shaking her head with concern.

"Don't cross a Stevens," she informed Katherine. "If you cross one of us, you cross us all." Beth meant it as a joke, but there was truth to it, and it only supported her theory that she had done right to walk away from Alistair early on in their affair. The last thing her career needed was the Stevens family's wrath.

Chapter 3

Katherine stood in the wings, watching the stage crew put the final touches in place for the opening act. Her mask was in place, her dress was a peach organza affair that floated around her like a cloud, and her thick ebony hair was scooped into a high and tight ponytail making her cheekbones look dramatic.

Because her co-host, Mason Stevens, was so tall, Katherine could wear her heels and not tower over him, making her more like Katherine, the model, and less like Katherine, the television host. There was a distinctive difference. One had to deal with large in-person audiences, and the other didn't.

"Hello, Katie," Alistair whispered in her ear, appearing from nowhere and without warning.

He was simply standing behind her, not touching her or even looking at her as he, too, watched the action on the stage. From afar, they would look like mere acquaintances.

"Hello, Al," she greeted back. He knew she hated the nickname Katie, and she knew he hated Al.

"I heard a rumor that you would be here this evening." Alistair smiled at one of the cute female stagehands who waved at him. "Should I tell her I'll be going home with you this evening and not to waste her time?"

"You're sure of yourself, aren't you?" Katherine couldn't suppress a smile.

"I'm sure of us, Katherine." Katherine could hear the smile in his voice. "You look delightful and smell divine." He inhaled deeply.

"I wish I could say the same, but since you snuck up on me, it's hard to tell." Katherine's heart rate sped up at the compliment given to her in his posh English accent. She loved his accent.

"I want to kiss you, Katherine," he whispered, his breath brushing her ear and making her whole body break out in goose pimples.

At that precise moment, as if the gods were on his side, the cute stagehand brushed against him and pushed him into Katherine as he did his best to avoid direct contact with the stagehand. He knew how the game was played nowadays, and an accidental brush today would be a sexual assault next week, especially when you were a wealthy earl.

He knocked Katherine harder than she expected, and it caused her to lose her balance, but his hand was there on her waist, holding her steady as he pulled her against him while the girl apologized and then scurried off into the shadows.

"No harm done," Alistair said as he held onto Katherine, letting his hand wander to her hip.

"No, no harm done," Katherine agreed, as she brushed at her skirt while peaking up at him.

His raven black hair was long and curled around his head, he was clean-shaven, and his blue eyes were as shocking as ever.

Why did he always have to make her so weak-kneed?

"So, tonight? Same place, same time?" he asked in a low, urgent voice as he stepped away from her.

Katherine nodded, knowing she didn't have the strength to say no.

"There you two kids are!" Mason said as he threw his arms over both of their shoulders. "Planning the wedding yet?" he asked with a grin.

"Katie turns me down every time," Alistair said in a bored voice.

"Perhaps it's because you call me Katie, Al?" Katherine said in an equally bored voice.

They stared daggers at each other, which was part show and part sexual tension. It was how they always behaved around each other. The first time Katherine had seen Alistair in public around his family after their affair had started, she had been taken aback by his abrupt, almost rude behavior, but then she realized that it was a defense mechanism to shield her and himself from his prying family.

"No fighting, children," Cassandra said as she joined her husband.

"You could cut the sexual tension with a knife!" Mason whispered to Cassandra in a not-so-subtle whisper.

"That's gross, Uncle Mason!" Mave, who had also joined them, whispered back.

"But true," he insisted as he pushed the curtain aside and looked into the audience, Cassandra and Mave joining him.

Alistair reached out and grabbed Katherine's hand while they were all distracted, rubbing her palm with his thumb before trailing his fingers up the inside of her arm before stepping away.

"I hope you all break a leg tonight," Alistair said before he turned and walked away without looking back as Beth joined him, linking her arm through his as they went to find their seats.

"Everyone but Lizzy is here this evening, even Trisha," Cassandra said as she stepped away from the curtain.

Trisha Livingston was one of the wealthiest women in the city and Lizzy Stevens's best friend from college. She and Lizzy handled the production of the show every year. Without them, it wouldn't happen, and the money wouldn't be raised for the Foster's for College program.

The show was a Stevens family tradition, and Katherine always wondered why they were all so involved, but she had never had the chance to ask.

They heard the orchestra start warming up.

"Showtime!" Mason said as he took Katherine by the hand, suddenly all business. "Let's go over a few things before we start."

*****

Five hours later, Katherine was sitting on the bed in her hotel room, brushing her wet hair as her mind raced through the show that had miraculously gone off without a hitch. Mave's narration had, by far, been the funniest thing that Katherine had seen in a long while. What would have been a boring mime act had become a rollicking farce.

The woman was fast on her feet and with a comeback; at one point, she had been chased. There had even been a pie that Mason had snuck on stage for her to throw at the actor involved, but in the end, they had played nice for the audience and parted with a handshake. Of course, after they were off stage, it was a completely different matter, but the Stevens had circled the wagons, and the actor had slunk away, unable to match the united front before him.

Katherine caught her reflection in the mirror across from her and grimaced. Without her makeup and hair styled, she looked plain.

When the knock on her door came, it startled her even though she was expecting it.

Taking a deep breath, she stood and laid her hairbrush on the dresser with a shaking hand. She knew it was Alistair and what was about to happen. She shouldn't have washed her makeup off, but she always did. Perhaps it was her way of testing his sincerity. If it was, he had passed every time.

"Who is it?" Katherine asked through the door.

"It's Alistair, Katherine." She could hear the amusement in his voice.

Slowly she opened the door and caught her breath once more at the beauty of the man. He had lost his bow tie, his top buttons were undone, his suit jacket was over his arm, and his sleeves were rolled up, showing his muscular forearms.

Katherine lost herself as she rested her head against the open door and dreamily sighed while she took in his mussed hair and bright blue laughing eyes. Alistair was always happy and laughing. It was one of the things she loved most about him.

"Are you going to invite me in, beautiful?" Alistair asked, his voice husky.

Katherine blushed at the compliment.

"I'm glad to see that," he said as he reached up and stroked her red cheek.

They both froze at the simple connection, their eyes locking as the electricity between them spiked.

"I missed you," Alistair whispered.

"I missed you too," Katherine whispered back, and then they were in each other's arms, making up for the year apart. When they kissed, it was as if time didn't exist. They could have been together only yesterday.

******

When Katherine awoke in the small hours of the morning, she found Alistair sitting in a chair, watching her sleep.

"What's wrong? Why are you watching me sleep? It's creepy, Alistair," Katherine pushed herself up in bed, wrapping the sheet around herself.

"I want you to marry me, Katherine," Alistair blurted out, ignoring her.

Katherine's heart skipped a beat as it always did when he proposed.

"We've been over this, Alistair. I don't want to get married, at least not yet." Katherine shook her head and bowed it so he couldn't see her.

"When then, Katherine? It's been nine years since we started this. Whatever this is, that's between us." He stood up and moved to sit beside her on the bed. "You say it's your career, but I don't think that's it anymore." He pushed the hair she was using to shield her face over her shoulder. "Do you love me?"

Katherine looked up at him with tears streaming down her cheeks. "I do." She nodded. Words of love and affection between them had never been a problem. He had told her early on that he loved her, and she had no trouble returning the words.

"Then what is it, Katherine?" His voice was soft.

She wanted to scream at him that he didn't get it, that when he won her and got to know her, he wouldn't really want her. He only knew part of her, not all of her. He didn't know the insecure, shy, and timid part of her.

Katherine wiped her cheeks. "I must go home. My mother is sick, and she needs me."

"I'm sorry to hear that, but it sounds like one more excuse, not the truth. Wouldn't she want to see you married and happy?"

Katherine couldn't take his intense stare and wiggled out of bed, reaching for her robe.

"She would, but my father wouldn't," she said without thinking and then cursed herself for letting it slip.

Alistair kept silent, willing her to continue, and she did, but not in the way he thought she would.

"In fact, this is probably the last time we will see each other. Once I go home, my father will want me to stay, and after my mother..." she couldn't finish the sentence. "Once I'm there, with no ally to help me escape. I'll be stuck."

"Are you saying your father holds you there against your will?" Alistair asked with disbelief.

Katherine knew he wouldn't believe her. He had a happy family and couldn't imagine anything else. It was hard to explain that her father was the master of guilt and held her against her will mentally, not physically. She was weak where he was concerned and always had been.

"Not physically." Katherine shrugged.

"I'm not going to pretend that I understand, but I have a simple solution." Alistair stood and walked towards her, placing his hands on her shoulders. "Marry me, then when the time comes, I'll come and get you as your husband."

Katherine closed her eyes. It would be the answer to a prayer, but she couldn't do that to Alistair.

"I can't use you like that, Alistair. I have never wanted to use you! Don't you understand that?" She pushed his hands off her shoulders.

"If you love me and I love you, how is it using?" He shook his head in confusion.

"Please," she fell on the chair behind her, covering her face with her hands in despair.

She was suitable for a private affair, but she would never measure up to being the wife of an English earl, but it was his normal, and there was no way he would understand her fear of failure where he was concerned.

"Fine, make me a promise then." Alistair knelt in front of her and took her hands in his. "When the time comes, you will do everything in your power to find me, and we will talk about this one last time, and I do mean last time."

Katherine met his eyes. Maybe she could get her head on straight by then. Perhaps she could find him and say yes. It was a promise she was willing to make, sure that it would hurt her more if she didn't keep the promise than it would hurt him.

She nodded, and he stood, pulling her into his arms.

"A kiss to seal the deal," he demanded, and Katherine complied.

Chapter 4

Katherine pulled back the heavy curtains in her mother's room to let in the morning light.

"Good morning, Mom," she greeted with a smile, doing her best to hide her despair at the sight of her mother's pale thinness. All her zing was gone.

"Good morning, sweetie," she greeted in a weary voice.

Katherine had been home for three agonizing months. Her mother, Dora, had been able to do more three months ago than she could now. She had still dined and sat with them in the evening then, but now she was too weak to get out of bed.

"What would you like for your breakfast this morning?" Katherine asked, moving to adjust the pillows behind her.

"Nothing, thank you. Just some tea." Dora started coughing uncontrollably, and Katherine, unable to help, stood by with a handkerchief in case she needed it.

The hardest part was not being able to help. Katherine could fetch and carry and keep her mother company, but she couldn't help her. Dora was never going to get better, and it broke Katherine's heart.

"Are the girls around today?" Dora asked as she always did.

The girls were Katherine's younger sisters. There were three of them, and they avoided the sick room as much as possible, so Katherine had taken to telling Dora that they were away most of the time.

"I'm not sure. I haven't seen them today, but I'm sure they are because Dad's guests start to arrive today." Katherine's father, George Randolph, was determined to carry on as if nothing was amiss in his life, and he didn't have a dying wife.

"That's nice. The girls will enjoy all the company. I hope you get to spend some time with everyone." Dora started coughing once more. "Who knows," she gasped, "maybe someone will recognize you."

Katherine gave a small smile. Very few people recognized her outside of certain New York social circles. She had never used the name Randolph for work. She used her mother's maiden name Rhodes, and the small, coastal South Carolina community where they lived, didn't have much use for high fashion. Katherine's sisters hadn't a clue about her career because they didn't have much interest in Katherine since she was ten years older than the oldest.

"I doubt it, Mom. Besides, I'm going to hang here with you. I thought we could binge-watch Lost again. We haven't seen it since it came out years ago."

"Katie, you need to spend time with other people, too," her mother admonished.

"I've spent the last ten years going to parties. I can miss a few now." Besides, it was her father's attempt to find husbands for his youngest daughters. George had no hope for Katherine in that department.

The thought made her immediately think of Alistair, and she grew sad, which must have been reflected in her expression.

"You're sad again. Are you thinking of him?" Dora asked, watching her daughter closely.

"Yes," Katherine agreed as she moved toward the door. "I'll get your tea."

In a moment of weakness, when her mother had been fading, Katherine had told her about the man she loved. She hadn't mentioned specifics or a name, only that she had fallen madly in love. She had wanted her to know him, even if it was in a vague way.

Dora's room was off the kitchen and overlooked the garden. Katherine's room was next to it, and a bathroom connected the two rooms, making caring for her mother easier.

"Good morning, Miss Katie. How is your mother this morning?" Abigail Just, the housekeeper, asked.

"About the same, Ms. Just. She only wants tea this morning." Katherine started the kettle for the water.

"I'll make a few pieces of buttered toast. It won't hurt, will it?" Ms. Just said as she moved around Katherine to start the process.

Ms. Just was a tall, thin woman with snow-white hair who had worked for her family since Katherine was a girl. She kept her own counsel and didn't tell tales or gossip; Katherine greatly respected her.

"What would you like for your breakfast?" she asked Katherine.

"I had mine hours ago," Katherine said with a calm smile because it was expected of her.

Katherine only had a few hours of the day to herself in the early morning, and she valued them because they gave her a chance to reflect on who she was and wanted to be.

"Did you want to go over the menus for tonight's dinner in about an hour?" Ms. Just asked.

"Sure, do the flowers still need to be arranged before the guests arrive?" Katherine asked as she dunked the tea bag into the hot water. "I can arrange them during Mom's nap if it helps," she offered.

"That would be lovely. You have a way with them that no one else does," Ms. Just said as she smeared butter on the toast that Dora probably wouldn't touch.

"Thank you. Have you seen the girls yet? Mom is asking for them."

"No, but when I do. I'll let them know." Ms. Just said as she avoided meeting Katherine's eyes. She knew that the likelihood of getting the girls to spend some time with their mother was nil.

"You're a treasure, Ms. Just. I couldn't do it without you." Katherine smiled at her once more as she picked up the tray and carried it across the kitchen to her mother's room.

******

Two hours later, having read the paper and gone through the mail from the day before with her mother, Katherine returned the tray to the kitchen when Ms. Just informed her that the flowers were in the drawing room when she was ready.

"Would you like to review the menus now?" she asked Katherine, taking in her exhausted appearance.

Katherine nodded. "Yes, I think I'll also cut a few roses for mother's room."

Dora loved roses, and they would brighten her room.

"That's a good idea. Would you like me to have Stan do it for you?" Ms. Just asked. Stan was the gardener, and Katherine had always wondered if he and Ms. Just had an intimate relationship as well as a working one.

"No, thanks. I think I prefer to do it myself." Katherine pulled up a stool from the corner of the kitchen and sat at the counter where Ms. Just had laid out the menus for that evening and the entire week. "It makes me sad. Mom should be doing this." Katherine swallowed back the tears that were always close to the surface as she ran her hand over the paper as if it would wipe away the sadness.

Ms. Just laid a comforting hand on her shoulder for a moment, then pulled up another stool.

They had been well into it for half an hour when her father arrived in the kitchen without warning.

"There you are, Katie! I've been looking all over for you!" It came out as an accusation.

"I'm putting the menus for the week together, Dad. Did you need something?"

George looked over her shoulder, looking at Katherine's choices. "No, I don't want what you've planned this evening. We need to go big. We only have a few very important people here tonight, and we need to impress them." George insisted. "Your mother can handle it."

"No, Dad, she can't," Katherine softly said. She knew her father hadn't seen Dora in a few weeks since he had been traveling, maybe even longer.

Katherine watched his jaw flex either in impatience or distress, but Katherine couldn't be sure which. Dora and George's relationship had always been a mystery. They were more partners than husband and wife, and Katherine had never seen a moment of genuine affection pass between them in her lifetime.

"Fine, but it needs to be bigger!" he insisted once more. "My first guests have already arrived, and we're going to talk business in my study. I don't want to be disturbed. Would you let the girls know that they are here, that they should look their best, and be ready to help me entertain our guests this evening!" It wasn't a request, and Katherine nodded her agreement.

"I can help entertain as well, Dad," Katherine offered. She didn't know what devil had made her do it. Perhaps she was testing the waters to see if anything had changed over the years she had been away.

George took in Katherine's appearance, noting her old jeans and t-shirt and how her hair was piled sloppily on her head. "No, I need you to ensure everything is running smoothly behind the scenes. The girls will handle the guests."

It didn't upset Katherine in the past when he would push her into the shadows because it used to be his wife he would show off, but now it was his other three daughters, and it stung that she wasn't good enough. Either way, it had never been Katherine, and it never would be. She had to accept it.

"If only he knew!" Ms. Just exclaimed as she closed the menu folder and stood after he had left the room.

"Knew what, Ms. Just?" Katherine asked with a tilt of her head. The outburst was so unlike her.

"I know what you've been up to, Katherine Rhodes. Your mother tells me everything. I've watched all your shows and seen all your photos on the society pages of the papers has sent to her. You put your sisters to shame.

You could run circles around them if given a chance." Ms. Just crossed her arms in a defensive action, and Katherine pushed back tears once more.

Who knew she had a champion in Ms. Just? It was unexpected.

Katherine stood and walked toward her, placing her hands on her shoulders.

"Thank you, Ms. Just. I needed to hear that, especially today." She leaned down and placed a kiss on her cheek.

"I think it's time you call me Abby," Ms. Just insisted.

Katherine nodded. "Would you mind calling me Katherine? I prefer it over Katie."

"Of course, it suits you much better," Abby agreed.

Stan, a big burly man with grizzly hair, banged through the door at that moment and looked at the two of them.

"Stan, we're calling Katie Katherine now!" Abby informed him.

"Fine by me. Do you have any coffee?" He asked as he sat on one of the stools the two women had vacated.

Katherine smiled at his simple response.

"You go see to those flowers, Katherine. I'll take care of the menu, maybe even ask your mother's advice just this one time. It might take her mind off things for a few minutes."

"Thank you, Abby." Katherine left the kitchen with a smile.

It was all about the little moments.

Chapter 5

Katherine did as her father requested and woke up her sisters, reminding them they needed to look in on their mother. She felt like Cinderella in the process, and it made her smile. Her sisters were all close in age. They were all petite, blond-haired, blue-eyed princesses, and not for the first time, Katherine wondered where she got her looks from.

Jessie was twenty-three, fresh out of college. Jillian was twenty-one and had just reached drinking age, and Jackie was nineteen and had just completed her freshman year at college. They were young and tan and thought they ruled the world with Daddy's money.

After waking the young girls and having pillows chucked at her head and a few choice words hurled at her, Katherine made her way to the rose bushes that lined the glass windows of the enclosed heated pool and solarium. It was almost time for lunch, and she needed to make sure that Abby didn't need her help, but first, she would cut some roses and take them to her mother.

She was halfway through cutting the roses while enjoying the warm room despite the chill outside and had moved around to the back of the bushes when she heard her sisters arrive in solarium.

"They're both so handsome! This is going to be fun!" Jillian said in a hushed tone, and it made Katherine smile. Katherine had been too shy to be boy-crazy. At least, she had been until she had met Alistair.

"I want the tall blond one. What was his name?" Jessie asked as she threw herself down on a lounger. She was wearing a daring bikini that was a bright pink and showed her young body off to its best advantage.

"Simon, I think," Jackie said as she settled down next to her sister. She was in a more conservative one-piece.

"I want the tall and dark one with the baby blue eyes," Jillian whispered in a rush as she looked over her shoulder. Then she smiled at someone Katherine couldn't see before she walked over to the pool and dramatically dropped her wrap, revealing a white two-piece.

Katherine would never have the guts to put on such a display as that.

Yes, she was used to modeling clothes, but it was always about the clothes, not about the body in them. With all three girls, it was about the body.

"Won't you join us?" Jillian asked, her voice dropping a few octaves as she tried to become a seductress.

"No, thank you, I'm enjoying the view for now," a man with a southern drawl responded.

Katherine waited for her sisters to offer the guest a drink or something to snack on, and when after a few minutes of stilted silence, it didn't happen. She felt obliged to take over, no matter what her father said.

Taking her courage in hand as she looked at her frayed jeans and old t-shirt, she stepped out from behind the bush with a pleasant smile, but her smile faded as she saw a familiar pair of blue eyes look over at her.

Tall, dark, and handsome definitely described Alistair Stevens.

Katherine took in Alistair's appearance as he took in hers. He looked relaxed in a pair of slacks and a dress shirt with the top button undone and the sleeves rolled up, but he was missing his usual smile. He looked serious and didn't look as if he was surprised to see her either.

He always had a smile for her, but not this time. He was acting the same way he did when his family was around, indifferent.

"Hello!" the tall, handsome blond man greeted. "Who are you, the gardener?"

Katherine smiled and opened her mouth to introduce herself, but a laughing Jillian cut her off before she could.

"That's our big sister, Katie," she introduced. "Katie, this is Simon Black and Alistair Stevens. They're here as father's guests."

"Hello," Katherine smiled at them, "can I get you something to drink or a snack? Lunch should be ready in about half an hour." She was proud that her voice came out sounding normal. It was better if she acted as if he had never met Alistair and kept her guard up. It would raise too many questions with her sisters. Then the mocking would begin. Plus, if the way he was treating her was anything to go by, that was the way he wanted to pay it too.

"Are you sure I don't know you from somewhere?" Simon asked.

"No, I don't think so," Katherine's smile grew tense as she let her gaze look over Alistair one more time, waiting to see if he would respond or join in on the conversation.

"I think we're fine, Katie," Alistair replied seriously, giving nothing away.

Katherine nodded, then turned and headed toward the door to the house. She was halfway across the patio with all eyes on her when she was passed by a beautiful brunette who dropped some papers when she bumped into Katherine.

"I'm sorry," the young woman laughed as they both bent down to pick them up, pausing when she looked at Katherine. The woman was lovely. Her hair was coiled at her neck, her white linen suit was fit to perfection, and her makeup was professional.

"There you are, Nadine." Alistair interrupted her as she was about to say something, kneeling to help them pick up the papers. "Do you have a moment to review a few things?"

Nadine turned her stunned gaze to Alistair and nodded.

"Is there somewhere we can talk in private, Katie?" Alistair asked as he reached for the papers in Katherine's hand, and she caught her breath as their eyes locked when they brushed hands.

"Sure, follow me." Katherine gave a tense smile as she watched Alistair hand Nadine the papers and then place his hand on the small of her back to direct her to follow Katherine.

They looked perfect together. Who was she?

******

Alistair watched Katherine as he closed the door to the little sun room leading off the parlor as she left him and Nadine. She took the smell of fresh roses and something that was distinctively her when she left.

"Alistair!" Nadine hissed. "Is that who I think it is?"

Alistair looked at his excited assistant and suppressed a grin, keeping his usually serious countenance.

"Who do you think it is?" he asked, placing his hands in his pockets.

"That's Katherine Rhodes. Why is she here in Charleston?" Nadine put her hands to her hot cheeks.

Nadine was an interesting woman that Alistair had yet to figure out completely. She was lovely to look at and very sweet, but she was drawn to beautiful women like a moth to a flame. They had never discussed her sexuality because it wasn't a proper work conversation, but it wasn't hard to figure out.

Nadine also lived and breathed fashion. All her vacations and extra money were spent on attending fashion shows all over the world. If runway models had the equivalent of baseball cards, she would have the collection. Unbeknownst to Nadine, Alistair had kept up with Katherine's whereabouts via Nadine's chatter.

"She looked lovely, didn't she? I swear she doesn't even have to try." Nadine sighed as she sat on a chair and sorted through the pile of papers that were now a jumbled mess. "I swear, I don't know why Randolph can't use and computer like everyone else."

"Perhaps Ms. Rhodes is incognito. Did you think about that? Not everyone wants to be recognized." Alistair watched Nadine pause at the thought.

Alistair had no idea if that was what was going on or not, but he knew he didn't want Simon to recognize Katherine for selfish reasons. Simon was about climbing the social ladder, and a famous runway model would help his cause. He wouldn't let up, making Alistair's goal of learning more about Katherine during his brief visit difficult.

Alistair's reason for meeting with George Randolph was to learn more about Katherine. She had hinted that her problems stemmed from her father, so perhaps meeting the man would answer a few of his questions since Katherine wasn't inclined to do it.

George Randolph was hosting a party of investors to see which firm would get to take on his vast fortune. Alistair didn't care if they got the account one way or the other, but Simon was eager, which could make things tricky.

"Is that why you pulled me in here?" Nadine asked, her eyes growing wide. "But then you would know all about that kind of thing coming from such a famous family, wouldn't you?" Nadine nodded her head. "I got you!" She made a motion like she was zipping up her lips and throwing away the key. "Incognito."

Alistair nodded his agreement. "I'll see you at lunch. I have something to do," he said as he left Nadine sorting through papers with a smile on her face.

Chapter 6

Katherine had taken the roses to her mother, who was still sleeping. She took a minute to watch her before she forced herself to place the flowers where she would see them when she woke up and left the room.

It was much later, after lunch, when she finally got around to arranging the rest of the flowers. She was in the dining room working on the centerpiece when her father joined her, and his face looked like thunder.

"I told you to ensure the girls looked nice for our guests! They showed up to lunch in their swimsuits and wraps." his voice was low but fierce.

Katherine was surprised they had bothered with the wraps. "I told them your wishes when I woke them this afternoon, Dad. I don't know what more I could have done," she insisted, keeping her eyes on the flowers.

"It's your job to keep them in line!" he growled.

"No, that's your job. You're their father, not me. Plus, I've been a little busy this morning." Katherine held up a flower. "Why don't you have them help around here? It might be good for them. You were unhappy with the way I handled the menus. Perhaps one of them could take over that." Katherine doubted they would know how to do such a minor thing. They would probably all be eating salads for every meal.

"When I want your advice on how to run my house, I'll ask for it!" George was turning red at Katherine's unusual directness, so she didn't feel it was the right time to remind him that it was her mother's house, not his. It had been something Dora had brought into the marriage, along with a tidy inheritance.

"All right, Dad," she agreed, not knowing what else she could say to calm him down.

"Stop calling me Dad. I want you to call me George from now on!"

The silence between them was heavy as Katherine laid down her flower and clutched the table in front of her for support. Why would her father suddenly want her to call him George and not Dad? Was he that ashamed of her?

"Why?" Katherine's voice was soft but steady.

"Why doesn't matter? Just do as I ask!" Then he turned and stalked out of the room, leaving a pale Katherine behind him.

Katherine walked on unsteady legs through the dining room to the parlor, her mind a jumbled mess. She was proud of her moment of backbone, but she had never dreamed it would cause her father to demand she stop calling him Dad. She looked out the window with a view of the massive lawn in front of the house. If it was a lovely evening, the windows opened and created an opening to the lawn. It was a great advantage for parties, but Katherine didn't see the view.

As usual, when something unpleasant arose, she started to think about everything but the thing that was troubling her most. Now she thought about what would happen when her mother was gone. Would her father sell the house? She would miss the house if he did.

"Maybe you're wrong?" Alistair's voice spoke behind her, where he was sitting in a chair near the large fireplace.

It startled her, and she spun around to face him. How had she forgotten he was around? It had never happened before. Was she finally losing her mind?

"Excuse me?" Katherine looked at him, hoping he hadn't just heard the conversation between her and her father, knowing he had.

"If he doesn't want you to call him Dad, maybe he will let you go when the time comes." Alistair stood, walking toward her. "Although, I do admit it is an odd request." He frowned in thought.

She hadn't even begun to process her father's comments, much less think of what they meant long-term., but it was obviously something that Alistair was willing to do for her.

"What are you thinking?" Alistair was serious as his attention focused on her, and he reached out to touch her pale cheek. His tender touch made her want to cry.

"I'm thinking that I'll miss this house when he sells it," Katherine turned to look out the window.

"Buy the house then," Alistair suggested.

"Alistair, I don't have that kind of money!" Katherine shook her head. She had enough to live frugally for the rest of her life, but not if she dropped four million for a house.

"Yes, you do." Alistair dropped his hand. "Remember that money you gave me six years ago to invest for you?" He crossed his arms and watched her.

"I did that so that I would always have a reason to talk to you, not because I expected to make more money with it," Katherine explained.

"That's nice to hear but also a bit insulting at the same time." He paused as he thought about her comment. "Either way, the result is that I did make you some money," Alistair told her, a sum that made her gasp.

"How? Why didn't I know? Oh my God, am I going to jail for tax fraud!" She didn't know about the money, had never reported it. It was her mind once again thinking about something other than what was really bothering her.

Alistair stared at her with a shocked expression. "You really do like to make mountains out of molehills, don't you?"

Katherine didn't hear his comment as her mind spun. It was too much! First, her father, now Alistair. This was him getting to see the real her whether she wanted him to or not as she started to have a panic attack.

"I have to sit down." She crossed her legs, sat on the floor between the table and the window, and bowed her head down while resting her hands on the back of her neck.

"Okay," Alistair said, joining her on the floor and watching her patiently as she took deep breaths to calm her nerves.

He sat across from her for a few minutes, waiting for her to calm herself. When she looked up at him with tears, he reached for her hands and held them in his own while he rested his forehead against hers.

"Oh, my love, this, whatever it is, goes very deep, doesn't it?" he asked, finally grasping how truly messed up her life was.

"You have no idea," her voice broke, and she closed her eyes, loving the feel of his warmth.

"Do you remember the first time I met you?" His voice was almost a whisper.

Katherine smiled and sighed. "I'll never forget it." It was a happy memory to focus on for a moment.

"Beth said something that I dismissed at the time and shouldn't have." He squeezed her hands as if asking for forgiveness for what he was about to say.

"What?" Katherine licked her lips nervously, and Alistair placed a tender kiss on them before he rested his head against hers once more.

"Beth said to be careful, that she didn't know much about you, and you were a good woman, but you might be a bit broken." Alistair caressed her cheek as Katherine felt the tears start.

"She's right. You should be careful and stay away from me because I am broken."

"That's not what she meant. Our family has its fair share of broken, and we excel at helping each other glue the pieces back together." Alistair gave a gentle smile as he squeezed her hands once more. "She didn't want me to hurt you."

"You could never hurt me, Alistair. I know that you would sooner hurt yourself." Katherine automatically defended him.

"I'm glad you think that, but I'm human and it's inevitable that I eventually will hurt you. My question for you is do you know how much you hurt me every time you walk away and choose not to share?" Alistair's voice broke.

Katherine shook her head. "No, put it proves that you should stay away from me because I do."

"No, I want to help you figure out what needs to be fixed so that you will stop hurting me. Will you let me help you?" He stood up and offered her his hand. Katherine knew if she accepted it, she would have to put all her cards on the table and hope he was still willing to love her afterward.

Katherine was about to take his hand when she heard her father's voice.

"Why are you on the floor, Katherine?" George's voice sounded reasonable enough, but Katherine could see the muscle in his jaw jumping when she glanced up at him.

"I-" Katherine stared at him, voiceless, too cowed by his presence to say anything. She was once again the scared ugly little girl who only wanted his approval.

"It's my fault," Alistair said, his hand still outstretched toward her. His eyes met hers, asking her to trust him, and this time Katherine reached up and took his hand.

Neither one offered any more explanation than that as Katherine stood and crossed her arms.

"Alistair, I was looking for you. Do you have a moment to answer a few questions that I have?" George looked away from Katherine and placed his hand on Alistair's shoulder as he attempted to turn him away from her.

"Katherine?" Alistair asked, watching her.

Katherine tucked some hair behind her ear and licked her lips again, enjoying the way Alistair followed the movement despite her father standing right next to them.

"I have to finish the flowers and check on my mom." Katherine motioned toward the dining room.

"I hope I get the chance to meet her while I'm here," Alistair smiled at the prospect.

"That won't be possible. She's very ill. Let's go to my office and talk." This time George did manage to turn Alistair in the right direction, but not before he shot Katherine an angry look over his shoulder.

Katherine watched Alistair walk away with her father and wanted to call him back, and he must have sensed it because he turned and walked back toward her, taking her hand and leaning in to speak softly into her ear.

"I'll catch up with you later. We still have to talk. You have a lot to tell me." He let his lips brush her ear, smiled like her Alistair, then turned and joined her father, his serious expression back in place.

Katherine held fast to the fact that he had sensed her need and returned to her.

He was her Alistair still, but would he remain so when he knew Katie?

Chapter 7

Katherine's day went from bad to worse. Her mother's breathing grew labored, and Katherine begged and pleaded with her to go to the hospital, but she refused. Dora was adamant that they had all they needed and that the moment would pass.

It did, but dinner was over by the time Dora was sleeping fitfully.

Katherine asked Abby to sit with Dora and let her clean the kitchen. It took some coaxing, but they both needed a break from what they were doing and Abby needed to rest her weary feet. Katherine had placed the last piece of China in the cabinet when he heard laughter coming from the drawing room.

It made her wander down the hallway to a shadowed area by the stairs where she watched her sisters, father, Alistair, Simon, and Nadine sipping drinks and talking among themselves.

Katherine took a few minutes to watch Nadine and Alistair standing beside each other, talking with George. They looked perfect together, and Katherine wondered, for the hundredth time that day, what their relationship was exactly. Katherine felt something turn in her stomach when Jillian joined the little group and linked her arm with Alistair's.

It was the final straw on a horrible day, and she couldn't take it any longer, so she stepped forward into the room. She knew she was a mess. Her hair had tumbled down long ago, her t-shirt had water splattered on it, and her jeans were stained with flower pollen and cough medicine.

Alistair immediately broke loose from Jillian and took a step toward her as if he was going to catch her if she fell, which meant she must look worse than she felt, and Katherine shook her head, telling him to stop.

"I thought I would let you all know that Mom is through the worst and resting." Katherine knew they had all been oblivious to her mother's struggles that evening as they ate their dinner and drank their wine, but if they had any concern for Dora, she wanted to see it.

The girls all looked anywhere and everywhere but at her, and George forced a smile as his eyes shot daggers at Katherine.

"Thank you for letting us know, Katie. I knew she was in capable hands with you," he raised his glass, and everyone but Alistair followed his example.

"Thanks, Dad," she sarcastically drawled, turned on her heel, and walked out.

What had been the point? All it had done was upset her more. It had gotten Jillian away from Alistair, but only temporarily. She wanted to storm out and say to hell with all of them, but then her mother would be alone, and she couldn't do that to her.

When she got to the end of the hallway, just outside the kitchen door, she leaned against the wall, taking deep breaths and blinking rapidly to fight back the tears.

"It really is you, isn't it? Katherine Rhodes!" Nadine said in an excited whisper as she suddenly popped up only inches from Katherine's face. "You're so beautiful!"

"Ummm," Katherine's eyes grew wide, unsure how she should handle the situation.

"It's all right. You don't have to say a word. Alistair told me all about you being incognito. He knows all about that kind of stuff. I did want to get you alone to let you know that I am one of your biggest fans, and I'm super excited to meet you!" Nadine grabbed her hand and started pumping it while Katherine stared mutely at her. Was she crazy?

"Between you and me, I don't think Alistair wants Simon to know who you are." Nadine looked over her shoulder when she heard footsteps.

It was Alistair, and he was headed directly for them.

"Why doesn't he want Simon to know who I am?" Katherine asked in a normal voice, and Nadine hushed her.

"He's shy." Nadine smiled, and Katherine choked on her disbelief. "It's either that or he's jealous?" Her voice sounded thoughtful as she watched Alistair walk toward them.

"Nadine, I told you-"

"Incognito, I know." Nadine nodded her head in agreement. "But I just had to tell her I was a fan." She looked over at Katherine, who was staring at Alistair with confusion.

"I think Katherine has had enough for one day," Alistair looked at her with concern.

Katherine nodded and stood, wobbling a little from exhaustion and stress.

Alistair automatically reached for her. "When was the last time you ate?" he asked, taking in her parlor.

"About five," she frowned as she tried to recall.

"This evening?" Alistair asked as she placed an arm around her waist.

"No, this morning. I've been busy." Katherine rubbed her forehead. "I should check on Mom."

"No, you should eat and then get some rest." Alistair turned to Nadine, who was watching them with interest. "Nadine, would you please tell the others that I have received an important phone call and may not return this evening."

"It was nice to meet you, Nadine." Katherine gave her a weak smile.

Nadine nodded without comment, gave them one more curious glance, then turned and returned to the party.

"Now, where is the kitchen?" Alistair asked, taking most of Katherine's weight as he followed her directions and then sat her at the counter. "What would you like, a sandwich or an omelet?"

"What are you doing here, Alistair?" Katherine asked as she rubbed her face. "It's not just a coincidence, is it?"

Alistair smiled as he took some eggs from the refrigerator and began hunting for a pan.

"No, I went to Wyatt and asked him how I could find you. Once I assured him that my intentions were honorable, he willingly offered the information." Now, he was hunting for a spatula.

"So, your family knows about us now?" Katherine asked. Not that it mattered, she would probably never see any of them again.

Alistair stopped and looked at her. "Katherine, they have always known about us. I've never told them, but they are an observant bunch, and their track record is such that they figured it out long before we did."

"But why are you here?" He hadn't answered her question. He had told her how he had found her but not why.

"The next and final time I ask you to marry me, I want all the details so that I can counter any argument you might offer." He was hunting for something else now.

"After today, I thought you would run for the hills." Katherine sniffed, thinking about it.

"Where is the cooking spray?" Alistair asked.

"Excuse me, who are you, and what are you doing cooking in my kitchen?" Abby asked from her mother's doorway.

"Hello," Alistair said as he turned toward her. "I'm Alistair Stevens, the future Mr. Katherine Rhodes, or is it Randolph?" He looked over at Katherine, who had started to blush. "Katherine hasn't eaten since five this morning, so I was attempting to make her something before she falls over."

Abby looked at Katherine disapprovingly.

"You get out of the way before you ruin that nice suit. I'll make it. At the rate you're going, she'll die of starvation before you even get the eggs in the pan." Abby pushed him out of the way. "Katherine, you go lie down. I'll bring you a tray when it's finished."

"What about Mom," she asked, looking toward the door.

"She's still sleeping, and it's time for Stan's television shows. He's agreed to take the next few hours." Abby waved her toward her room.

"Would you be offended if I accompanied Katherine to her room Ms...?"

"You can call me Abby, and no, I wouldn't, seeing as you're the future Mr. Katherine." Abby looked between the two of them.

"I haven't said yes. In fact, I've said no several times now." Katherine objected weakly.

"Almost nine years, Katherine. You've said no for almost nine years now, and it hurts every time." Alistair looked at her, and it finally broke Katherine as she started to sob.

Alistair gathered her up and followed Abby's directions as he carried her to her room.

Chapter 8

Alistair had drawn Katherine a bath and helped her into it before retrieving the tray from Abby and serving her in the tub.

Usually, having Alistair as close as he was while she was doing something as intimate as bathing would have made her heart pound, but she was too tired to do anything but lay her head back and close her eyes as Alistair removed the tray from in front of her when she was finished.

"Let's talk about it," he insisted as he sat on the floor next to the tub and leaned his head back on the wall. He had removed his jacket and tie and rolled up his sleeves, and Katherine admired how his arms flexed as he crossed them across his chest. He was sitting at the foot of the bathtub facing her, so she had a clear view of his handsome face.

Katherine wondered what her sisters would do if they knew he was sitting with her while she had a relaxing bath. Of all their private moments together, this was the most intimate of them all.

"What's worrying you most, besides the most obvious, which is your mother?" Alistair reached over and turned on the tap to add a bit more hot water. "Is it your father, your sisters, the house?

Katherine shook her head, they all worried her, but once her mother was gone, she knew in her heart that all those things would be gone as well, so she was done fighting for them because it was like spinning her wheels or chasing her tail for no reason.

"Those hurt, but I've given up on most of them. When I returned, I was afraid that my father would want to keep me here, but now it's clear that once Mom is gone, he wants me gone as well. I'm just not sure why."

"Do you want to know what I think?" Alistair asked, his eyes meeting hers, conveying that if he told her the truth, it would add to the hurt.

She claimed that she didn't know why her father was pushing her away, but all of the pieces fell into place as she looked at Alistair. "Money," Katherine whispered, knowing the answer. She didn't want to make Alistair say it. It wasn't fair to him. She knew that George didn't want anyone around who could potentially fight him for the money, and the girls were too young and unworldly to have a clue. On the other hand, Katherine knew how the real world worked. Perhaps that was why he never wanted her to enter it.

Perhaps he wanted to keep her as clueless and dependent as her sisters.

"Money," Alistair agreed. "He doesn't have it yet, and I'm guessing he won't until your mother passes."

"What makes you say that?" Katherine closed her eyes at the pain of that fact. She was letting the tears escape and run hotly down her temples. It meant that he never loved Dora and had used her their entire married life. Her heart broke for her mother.

"Because he wants to invest but not until the summer." Alistair's voice was gentle.

Katherine nodded, understanding.

They were silent for a moment.

"Who exactly is Nadine?" Katherine finally asked. Needing to focus her thoughts on something else.

"You mean besides your biggest fan with stalker-like tendencies?" Alistair smiled. "She's a very shrewd woman who knows true beauty when she sees it. I bet she'd be jealous as hell that I'm sitting next to you while you're in the bathtub, naked."

Katherine lifted her head and looked at Alistair with wide eyes. "Funny, I thought the same thing about my sisters."

"That they would want to be sitting next to you while you're naked in a tub?" Alistair purposely misunderstood her to make her laugh.

"No, that they would like to be naked in a bath with you sitting next to them or vice versa." Katherine didn't laugh, but she smiled.

"How nice, but should I be worried about my physical safety? Are they likely to follow me into the bathroom?" Alistair asked with mock sincerity. "You don't have to worry about Nadine. I subtly told her to keep it in her pants." Alistair's smile turned into a grin at Katherine's shocked expression in reaction to his crude phrasing.

"I don't think you're using that phrase properly unless...." Katherine's eyes grew wide, and Alistair only shrugged.

"Sexuality is not a proper conversation for the workplace," he insisted.

"Then she works for you?" Katherine felt a little better. "She's lovely. I always wanted to be petite and well rounded instead of a skinny beanstalk."

"Yet, despite that very inaccurate description of yourself, I have always had difficulty keeping it in my pants when you're around." Alistair let his eyes linger over Katherine's body, which the water did nothing to shield, and

Katherine felt herself blushing like she always did when Alistair admired her.

Eventually, he took mercy on her and spoke. "We always want what we can't have, don't we?" It was a comment that was charged with meaning.

"Yes, until we get it, then we often don't really want it." Katherine nodded.

"Is that what you're afraid of, Katherine? That once I have you, I won't really want you?"

"Partly," Katherine agreed. "I also don't think I'll be able to measure up in your world. Your parents are the perfect earl and lady. I can't hold a candle to that." She shook her head slowly as she thought about marrying an earl.

"Do you know why we are involved in the Fosters for College program?" Alistair asked, leaning forward. Katherine had the feeling that the point he was about to make was an important one. "My mother was a foster child. Her parents died when she was very young. My grandparents and father supported the cause before they knew her. When it was discovered that she went to college because of the program, which ultimately led to her meeting my father, it became a program we could never abandon."

Alistair reached for her hand, which rested on the tub's side.

"She was born to be my father's wife and my mother, no matter her background. If you ask her, she will tell you that, in the end, that is all that matters. The rest is only window dressing. But if it helps you to agree to marry me, I'll give up the title." Alistair squeezed her hand.

"No! Then you really would grow to hate me!" Katherine surged upward out of the bath, reaching for a towel and wrapping it around her. "You don't need to change who you are. I do. I'm the one with the issues, and I know that. I just can't figure out how to deal with them." She walked into her bedroom and sat heavily on the bed.

Alistair followed her and stood across the room with his arms crossed as if it kept him from reaching out for her.

"I want to fix it all for you, Katherine. I want to handle your father, buy you this house, and hire around-the-clock care for your mother. I want to see you happy, and I would move heaven and earth to do that, but I agree with you, and I'm beginning to understand that none of the things I could do for you would help until you decide you want to be happy."

Alistair moved to the chair in the corner of the room where he had left his jacket and tie, picked them up, and then handed her a card.

"I can do this one thing for you. This is the company that will be sending a nurse to help with your mother. You have enough to pay for it. Wearing yourself out won't help you or her. The nurse should be here by now," he said, looking at his watch.

"When did you do this?" Katherine asked, looking at the card.

"There's always the time to do what you want to do," he vaguely answered as he walked toward the door.

"I'm done with putting myself out there, Katherine. It hurts too much when you push me away. If you change your mind, you can find me. But if you find me, Kathrine, you better be playing for keeps."

Katherine watched as he left, closing the door gently behind him.

Why did it feel like she had just lost him? She had never felt that before. In the past, there had always been the promise of next time.

Katherine put on her pajamas and went to check on her mother. Sure enough, a nurse was sitting with her. She introduced herself. They all talked for a few minutes, and then there was nothing to do but go to bed.

The feeling of loss would leave when she saw Alistair in the morning. She was tired, and her brain was playing tricks on her, but this reasoning didn't keep her from crying herself to sleep.

However, the following day, Alistair was gone. He had been called away on an emergency in the night, but Katherine knew there had been no emergency.

He had meant what he said. He was done.

Chapter 9

Katherine's mother died on a Saturday, six weeks later.

Despite her father's insistence that she remain until things were settled, as soon as the funeral was over, Katherine was on the first flight back to New York. There was nothing left for her in Charleston, and neither her father not her sisters needed her.

Upon her return, Katherine's first phone call was to Laura Stevens, her agent. The sooner she got back on the modeling circuit, the better. Thankfully Laura had something for her in Milan, Italy, the following week.

It was a challenging week. She had lost some weight which the designers loved. The consensus was the thinner the model, the better the clothes were featured. The work was just what she needed to forget about her mother and Alistair for a while.

Katherine had spent the last ten years running away from home and all that it represented, and that had defined her. Now that she didn't need to run, she wasn't sure about anything. She had lost her mother, who was her past, and she had lost Alistair, who had been her present, but what was her future?

Was it Alistair? Was it her career? Was it a one-bedroom walk-up with twenty cats?

After Milan, she headed to London to attend a production meeting for the show she hosted. It was a ghost hunter show. It featured a group of ghost hunters who traveled all over England investigating haunted houses and buildings. Katherine played the skeptic and was always ready with an eye roll when they found something. The viewers seemed to love it.

The only issue that crept up from time to time was the crew's desire to investigate the Earl of Pennington's estate in Kent, which belonged to Alistair Stevens and his family. It had almost been a go eight years earlier, but a family emergency had canceled the investigation, and it had never seemed to be an option after that.

"What about Hardd House in Kent? Do you think the Earl of Pennington would be up for it?" Robert Gore, the head investigator, asked as if reading Katherine's mind.

"It's worth a shot. Katherine, what are your thoughts?" KiKi Mann, the head of production, turned to her.

Katherine shrugged. "We can ask, but they've always put us off in the past, insisting that the house isn't haunted."

"That's just the reason we should investigate there. Can you imagine if we caught something!" Robert insisted, practically drooling.

"I'd like to catch the young earl, if you get what I mean," Susie Baker smiled at the thought.

"We get what you mean," J.D, the cameraman, shook his head. Susie was the youngest at twenty-three, and she was always looking for Mr. Perfect.

"You can talk to your agent. She's the aunt of the young earl, isn't she?" J.D. questioned Katherine.

"No, I cannot," Katherine shook her head. "If you want permission, you need to make an official ask through the proper channels. The Stevens are very particular about such things." They were sticklers for a contract, and she didn't want it to come across as if she was taking advantage of a friendship.

"You're no help!" Robert pouted as he leaned back in his seat.

"If you want it, schedule it first, then the others around it. Having a wide-open schedule will help. The family is very busy and travels quite a bit. If you allow them to name the date, it might go better than it has in the past." Katherine was unsure of why she was giving advice on the matter. It was the last thing she wanted to do. Wasn't it? She had to admit she would love to see the house.

They discussed it for a few minutes more, but Katherine remained silent, knowing she shouldn't have said anything in the first place. The meeting lasted another hour then she was off to the airport to fly back to New York.

Katherine had been away for almost a month, but now it was time to meet with her mother's lawyer and have the will read. As a beneficiary, she had to be present, and her father was chomping at the bit. She couldn't put him off any longer.

She was amazed that she had stood up to him for as long as she had.

******

Two days later, Katherine stepped out of the hired car and looked at the massive skyscraper in front of her. She was dreading seeing her family again.

Katherine didn't realize how elegant she looked with her hair neatly coiled and her loose-flowing linen pantsuit. She was wearing three-inch platform sandals, which made her tower over almost everyone around her.

She entered the cool lobby of the building, pushed her sunglasses on her head, and slung her large leather handbag over her shoulder. She knew she was going to the office on the twentieth floor, and she was so busy trying to read the plaque next to the elevator to see what the lawyer's name was that she didn't pay enough attention when the time came to enter the elevator which caused her to walk into a hard wall of muscle.

She looked up as she was spun around by her elbows and saw Alistair looking down at her without a trace of his usual grin as he stepped backward and out of the elevator.

"Katherine," was all he said.

Katherine went to reach for him, but the door closed, separating them. She tried to push the open button, but it was too late. She was already zooming upwards.

Had it been her imagination? Had she wanted to see him so desperately that she had turned a total stranger into him? No, he had said her name.

It had shaken her so much that she took a few minutes before entering the office with the name Bryce Stevens next to it. At least that explained why Alistair had been in the building.

The big question was how and when had Bryce Stevens become her mother's lawyer.

She entered the quiet oasis and gave her name to the receptionist, who escorted her into a conference room where her father, three sisters, and Bryce Stevens were sitting around a large table.

"I apologize for being late. I ran into someone I knew in the lobby." Katherine smiled politely at the table as she gracefully slipped into a chair. She was still so upset by her run-in with Alistair that she missed her father's frown and her sister's open-mouthed stares.

"Katherine," Bryce greeted.

"Mr. Stevens." Katherine nodded in his direction. He was a handsome man, just like his son. His dark hair had turned grey, but his blue eyes were just as shocking.

"Shall we begin? This will be short. The terms are clear and well-defined. Bryce looked down at a set of papers in front of him.

"Yes. I'm sorry that Katherine was late, and we have already taken up so much of your time." George said with a soothing smile at Bryce.

Katherine had been less than five minutes late, and she'd bet that Bryce knew whom she had run into in the lobby.

Bryce looked up from his papers and blankly stared at George until his smile faded, and he cleared his throat as if he was suddenly tense and uncomfortable. It was a fantastic sight, and Katherine was forced to look down at her hands to keep from smiling.

Bryce looked down at his papers and began to read in a dry voice.

Katherine felt all the color leave her face and then rush back as he heard the terms of the will. It appeared that her mother had ensured that Katherine was well cared for and protected even after she was gone.

"Are there any questions?" Bryce asked, leaning back in his chair and looking at everyone around the table. What he was thinking was a mystery.

Katherine's father's face had turned a disturbing shade of red. It was so red it was almost purple, and her sisters looked from one to the other, confused by it all, but it was clear to Katherine. She had the house and the money. She had everything.

"I was her husband! The husband always inherits!" George blustered, standing up and slamming his hands on the table. Everyone but Bryce jumped.

George turned to Katherine and pointed at her. "This is her fault. She influenced her mother, who was so ill she wasn't in her right mind." He turned sharply to Bryce. "You helped them. You're in it for the money, Stevens! Is Katherine giving you a cut?"

Katherine gave an unladylike snort at the thought and covered it with a cough. To someone like Bryce Stevens, Dora's will was a pittance.

"You may, of course, contest it, but I promise you it would be a waste of time and money. Mrs. Randolph was seen by a physiologist and found to be of sound mind when the will was made. Katherine had no inkling of what was in the will, nor did I have contact with Katherine during the drafting of this will." Bryce reached into a folder on the desk next to him, and he pulled out what Katherine guessed was an additional copy of the will and slid it across the table toward George.

"You'll need this to contest." Bryce leaned back in his chair.

"This isn't finished!" George grabbed the will and stormed out of the office, and a heavy silence descended.

"What does this all mean?" Jessie asked, speaking for all the girls.

"Nothing much will change for the three of you. You will continue to keep your allowance. The only difference will be that instead of going to your father when you want something, you will go to Katherine or someone she designates to oversee the estate." Bryce's voice was calm as he watched the girls looking at each other.

"Katherine?" Jillian asked, unsure. Not only was she now in charge of the family money, but looking as she did, she seemed a stranger to them.

"Don't worry about it, Jillian. Why don't you three catch up with Dad? I'll let you know when I figure it all out. All right?"

The girls looked at each other and then nodded as they stood.

"Thank you. Mr. Stevens," Jessie said before she led the way out of the conference room.

Katherine turned to Bryce. "Can we talk?"

"We can, but I'll give you a few moments to collect your thoughts before we begin," he said before standing and leaving her alone in the large empty room.

Chapter 10

Katherine stood and walked over to the windows to look at the view below in an absent-minded way. She had many questions about her mother and why she would leave everything to her. What was she missing? Her mother hadn't left any clues, and it was evident her father was just as shocked as she was by her mother's choice.

When did Dora meet Bryce Stevens, and how did he become her lawyer?

Yet, despite these questions, Alistair was uppermost in her mind. She had seen him for only a moment, but it had made her sure of one thing. She would never have enough of him. Every time they parted, it hurt, but it hurt more when she couldn't have him despite his nearness.

He was in New York, and she hadn't known he was here. Had he known she was in the city? Had he known she was coming to his father's office and left before she arrived to avoid seeing her? The thought almost brought her to her knees.

He hadn't smiled at her. He always smiled at her.

Katherine rubbed her forehead, where she felt a headache building.

She didn't care about the money, but she had to solve the problem because it was apparent that it was the root of all that was wrong in her life.

Based on her father's reaction to the will, money is probably what held her parents together, which meant her mother had all the power, but what did that mean for Katherine?

She had so many visions play through her head of all the times she had gone to her father for approval or love and been pushed away. He never pushed the girls away as he did her, but why? Why did he want her to call him George?

Katherine kept turning these questions over in her head, one after the other, without being able to reach a conclusion. She didn't know how long Bryce left her for, but when he returned, she was no closer to figuring anything out than when he had left her.

He motioned to a chair to her left, and Katherine took it, leaning forward with her hands on the table. It was the first time she had spent so much time in Alistair's father's presence, and it was hard for her to comprehend how this cold man had raised such a warm son.

Katherine was openly staring at him in wonder, and he lifted an eyebrow at her continued silence which made her blush.

"I thought you had retired," Katherine said after she had cleared her throat. He didn't show it if he thought it was an odd first question.

"I have. I only work for the family now, but it's still a full-time job." He leaned back in his chair as if he had all day, which put Katherine at ease. The tone of his voice and his English accent reminded her so much of Alistair.

"But my mother... how, why?" She shook her head in confusion.

Bryce studied her and determined how much he could or should tell her.

"Alistair recommended my services to her. He assured Dora that I would ensure everything turned out how she wished." Bryce's face was emotionless as Katherine's eyes grew wide in surprise.

"When did Alistair meet my mother?" Katherine asked, trying to remember a time that he could have.

"I couldn't say." Bryce shook his head.

"When did she draft the will?" Perhaps that would give her a hint.

Bryce pushed the will toward her and watched as she studied it. It had been notarized four weeks previously. That meant that Alistair must have met her when he had been at the house six weeks earlier.

But Katherine couldn't remember Bryce coming to the house or her mother leaving it.

"Did you meet my mother?" Katherine asked in a husky voice full of emotion at the thought.

"I did, and she was a delightful woman who loved all of her daughters very much." He gave a gentle smile at the thought of her mother.

"How, when?"

"Where there is a will, there is a way," he said vaguely.

"You sound just like Alistair!" Katherine huffed as she threw herself back in her chair.

Bryce grinned in response, and it changed him completely. Now she could see Alistair.

Alistair had said he wanted to fix it all and make her happy and would move heaven and earth to do it. Was this what it felt like to have someone take care of her just for the sake of it and not because they had to?

"Your son is a good man," Katherine's voice broke as she spoke.

"I'm glad to hear it. His mother will be glad as well." Bryce leaned forward, all business.

"Let's discuss the details so that you know what steps you need to take over the next few months with regard to allowances and such."

The next hour was spent reviewing all the documents and the decisions she would have to make.

"I know you are retired and only work for family, but will you continue to act as my lawyer and help me oversee this?" Katherine had been building the courage to ask him for the last hour.

"If you like," Bryce agreed.

"Yes, please." She couldn't hide the relief in her voice at his acceptance.

"We should plan to meet in the next few weeks after you've had time to deliberate and make a few decisions." He stood, ending the interview.

Katherine nodded, taking the card and copy of the will he handed her. "Thank you."

He led her out of the conference room and stopped short as soon as he cleared the door.

"Grace, Cassie," he greeted as he stepped aside so that Katherine could see whom he was greeting.

"Katherine, I believe you know Cassie, but it has been a while since you last met my wife, Grace," Bryce introduced.

Katherine had only met Alistair's mother twice. The first time was at the birthday party where she and Alistair first met, and the second was at a College for Fosters concert years earlier, but the two had never had a conversation.

"Mrs. Stevens, Cassie," she greeted.

"If you can call Cassie by her first name, you can certainly do the same for me," Grace smiled warmly.

"Grace," she conceded.

"We were about to meet Alistair for lunch, but we thought we would see if Bryce was available to join us. We'd love to have you join us too, Katherine," Cassie said cheerfully. "It's probably been some time since you last saw your son, Bryce."

"Yes, about two hours," Bryce said drily.

Anyone else would have been embarrassed by the mistake, but not Cassie.

"That's good. Wouldn't you like to see him again?" she insisted.

"Sure, give me about ten minutes, and I'll join you," Bryce walked away from the little group.

"What about you, Katherine? Will you join us as well?" Grace asked as she watched her handsome husband walk away.

Katherine could see the love in her gaze as she watched him. Did she look at Alistair like that?

"No, thank you. I already have an appointment." Katherine gave a tense smile, unsure how to extract herself from the situation.

"I was sorry to hear about your mother," Grace said. Her voice was so gentle that it made Katherine want to cry. "I'm sorry I never got a chance to meet her, but Alistair said she was a lovely lady."

Had Alistair talked about her with his parents?

"She was," Katherine agreed.

"Would you like us to give Alistair your love?" Cassie asked, changing the subject.

It was as if someone had turned a light on. The women were matchmaking. This was an attempt to get her to see Alistair.

Katherine could only smile. If she said yes, they would do it, which would be awkward at the very least, and if she said no, it would be awkward again.

"I thought I would find you two here," a deep voice said behind them. Katherine felt her heart leap and her face flush as he recognized Alistair's voice.

Katherine forced herself to turn and look at him, doing her best to keep her expression neutral and failing miserably as they stared at each other, neither saying a word.

"Come on, Cassie, let's go see what's keeping Bryce," Grace said, grabbing Cassie's arm and dragging her away.

"I'm sorry. They've never been very subtle." Alistair was staring at her.

"You didn't smile," was all she could think to say. "Earlier today, when we met, you didn't smile."

"Lately, I don't have much to smile about," Alistair said, crossing his arms to keep from reaching out. Katherine could sense that's what he wanted to do because it was what she wanted to do.

"I'm sorry I'm taking so long to figure it out." She bit her lip to keep from tears at bay.

"But you are trying?" his voice was urgent.

"I promise you, I am." They were silent again. "Thank you for helping my mother."

Alistair nodded his acceptance of her thanks but didn't speak.

"Wh-" Katherine was cut off.

"Are you ready, son," Bryce asked, walking towards him with Cassie and Grace following behind him with frowns.

"Sure," he agreed, unconcerned with whatever Katherine was about to say.

"Katherine, if you would like to make an appointment before you leave, they can help you at the desk," Bryce said before he escorted the small party out of the office.

Katherine felt the sudden need to try harder to solve her problems because she needed to see Alistair smile again.

Chapter 11

S ince the reading of the will with Bryce and her family, Katherine had met with Bryce twice about the details and tried contacting her father several times without much success.

She had texted her sisters and informed them that there would be no change to their allowances, and everything would remain the same. She had also decided to keep the house and told her sisters that they were free to come and go from it as they always had. She had not issued the same invitation to her father, and it had felt rebellious not to.

It was her monthly meeting with her agent, Laura Stevens, and since they were both in New York, they had decided to have lunch at a trendy and expensive New York restaurant. As usual, Katherine had taken her time with her appearance and was wearing an expensive blue wrap dress and killer heels with her hair in loose waves around her shoulders. One couldn't meet Laura Wren under-dressed.

When Katherine arrived at the restaurant, she was surprised to encounter her father and sisters in the foyer, waiting to be escorted to their seats. Her surprise wasn't that they were there as much as it was who they were with.

Trisha Livingston was standing next to her father with her arm linked through his.

Katherine smiled and nodded at her sisters before she turned to her father to offer the same smile which died on her lips at his cold reception.

"What are you doing here?" her father asked, looking at his other three daughters suspiciously, most likely thinking they had invited her.

"Hello, Dad," Katherine softly greeted as she did her best to hide her confusion at the fact that Trisha was standing next to her father. Trisha was an one of the wealthiest women in New York and her her husband had died many years before.

"I told you to call me George!" he murmured in her ear as she passed him. It still hurt.

"Sorry, George," she said, forcing a smile.

Trisha was closely watching them interact with each other, and there was an awkward pause where her father should have introduced her but didn't. It wasn't necessary, however, as Trisha stepped forward and placed a social kiss on Katherine's cheek.

"Katherine, it's nice to see you again. I was sorry to hear about your mother. Of course, I didn't know she was married to George."

"Thank you, Trisha," Katherine responded, playing the game and kissing Trisha on the cheek in return.

"Are you joining us? That would be lovely," Trisha smiled a sincere smile at the thought, and Katherine couldn't help but return it.

"No, I have a meeting with Laura." Both women turned to look at George to see his reaction to the news when he made an odd noise, only to find him watching them suspiciously.

"Why are you looking at us like that, George?" Trisha asked with a tilt of her head. She was more intrigued than she was upset at his distrust.

"You two know each other?" he questioned through gritted teeth.

"Yes, but it seems to upset you. Why?" Trisha was watching him, and it was clear that she didn't like what she was seeing as she watched a few different expressions cross his face.

George must have caught on to her sudden displeasure because he gave a big grin as if all was right with the world, and for the first time, Katherine could see how charming he could be when he wanted. It was a side of him that she had never witnessed before.

"I'm sorry," he laughed. "I was caught off guard seeing Katherine here and then finding out that you two know each other," he shook his head, his grin in place. "It's just a wonderful coincidence."

"Why didn't you invite her? You wanted me to meet your daughters. I take it she is your daughter?" Trisha asked, looking over at Katherine.

"Not by birth. She's my stepdaughter," George admitted jovially as if it were common knowledge and excused his not inviting her. There was a tense silence among them until Jessie broke it.

"Dad! What are you saying?' Jessie hissed as she stepped up toward him and grabbed his arm.

Katherine heard a sudden whooshing in her ears as what he said finally registered and she unconsciously clasped Trisha's arm for support. The room started to spin, and she felt like she was going to be sick. Trisha was a quick study and wrapped her arm around Katherine's waist.

"I need to use the powder room. Katherine, would you like to come with me?" Trisha asked, not waiting for an answer as she walked toward the powder room with Jessie on her heels.

Trisha got her there safely and sat her on a small bench along one wall before pulling out her phone and sending a quick text, then sitting next to her as Jessie paced, looking from one woman to the other with looks of shock and confusion alternating on her face.

A minute later, Laura and Beth entered, looking at an ashen Katherine.

"What's the SOS about?" Laura asked, looking at Jessie with a question.

"This is Jessie, Katherine's sister. Her father and two other sisters are being seated at our table."

"Stepfather," Katherine said, taking a deep breath and biting her lip to keep from crying.

"Where's Alistair? I don't suppose he's here?" Trisha asked, but Katherine didn't hear them. Her mind was in a total freakout as she wrapped her arms around her waist.

"Alistair?" Jessie asked, more confused as to why he would be there. "Alistair Stevens?"

"Yes, dear," Trisha said absentmindedly as she took Katherine's hand and patted it.

Beth sat on the other side of Katherine, looking upset as she looked at Laura, who pulled out her phone and sent a quick text.

"If he's near, he'll be here shortly." Laura crossed her arms but otherwise kept a neutral expression.

"You're Laura Wren!" Jessie said, her eyes growing wide, but no one paid her any mind.

"I didn't know!" Katherine said to herself, then looked at Jessie with tears. "Did you know?"

Jessie shook her head, tears forming in her own eyes at her sister's hurt.

Laura's phone rang, and she said something before putting it on speaker without anyone noticing as she gave a subtle nod to Trisha.

"Katherine, are you saying that until five minutes ago when your father decided to tell you in the foyer of a restaurant that you had no clue he wasn't your real father?" Trisha asked, summing up the horrible moment in one concise sentence. Neither Katherine or Jessie realized that Trisha was explaining what had just happened for Alistair who was on speaker phone.

Katherine shook her head, unable to speak. Everything in her life had been a lie! Why had her mother never told her? Suddenly, so much about her childhood made sense.

"Oh Katherine, I'm so sorry!" Beth said, taking her other hand.

"You said our table, Trisha. What does that mean?" Laura asked.

"I've been seeing George socially, and he wanted me to meet his daughters. When Katherine showed up, he thought she was here to meet us, and by the look he threw at Jessie and her sisters, I think her thought they invited her." Trisha patted Katherine's hand again.

"But we didn't, and we didn't know that he hadn't invited Katherine for sure. He's still mad at her, so we thought there was a chance he hadn't." Jessie bit her lip, thinking she had said too much.

Hearing the words made Katherine start crying. The man she thought of as her father, wasn't, and he didn't want her in his life.

"Why is he mad at her?" Trisha asked. She was never afraid to ask a nosy question.

"Because mother left everything to Katherine and nothing to him like he thought she would," Jessie whispered as she started to cry too.

"Oh my!" Beth said as she started to cry and wrapped an arm around Katherine's shoulders.

The door opened, and a white-haired woman looked at the three crying women and then excused herself, saying something about using the family bathroom before bumping into someone standing behind her.

A moment later, Alistair was standing in the middle of the restroom with Cassie and Mason, trying to squeeze in as well. It would have been comical if there wasn't so much crying.

Jessie stopped crying and hiccuped as she saw Mason and Cassie join the serious group.

"You're Mason and Cassandra Stevens," she said in awe.

"Yes, dear," Trisha said, standing to make room for Alistair, who took her place next to Katherine.

"My whole life has been a lie," Katherine whispered before she buried her head in Alistair's suit-covered shoulder and started sobbing.

"Come along, Jessie. Let's go back to your father," Trisha said as she took the girl's arm in hers.

"I don't want to," Jessie whispered as she looked at her sobbing sister.

"You will join us as if nothing is wrong for your sister's sake, Jessie. These five will help Katherine pull it together, and they will go and have lunch as if nothing is wrong." Trisha opened the bathroom door. "Wyatt, Davis," she greeted, sweeping past them.

In other circumstances, it would have amused Katherine that Wyatt and Davis were respectful enough to stay out of the lady's room but Mason and Alistair had no such worries.

"Would you all leave Katherine and me alone for a moment, please?" Alistair asked.

"Yes, Mason will use his considerable charms to get an out-of-order sign placed on the door. You both take your time." Cassie said, placing a kiss on Katherine's head. "We're also going to ask for a table in the middle of the restaurant." She looked at Alistair, letting him know what was expected.

He was expected to help Katherine and get her to the table where her father could see her having lunch with them as if nothing was wrong.

Beth wiped her eyes and squeezed Katherine's hand once more before she stood and quickly fixed her face in the mirror, then followed the others out of the room.

Katherine didn't notice any of it in her misery.

Chapter 12

Alistair sat in silence as Katherine cried on his shoulder. Her sobs had turned to a gentle weeping, and still, Alistair said nothing. When the weeping turned to sniffles, he handed her a handkerchief and waited while she mopped her face. He watched her carefully when she stood and walked toward the mirror to fix her makeup.

Katherine studied her reflection. Her face was familiar, but who was looking back at her? She had always assumed it was pieces of her mother and George, but now it was a stranger. Someone she had never met was her father. Did she look like him? Was he even alive?

"You don't have to figure it out today or even tomorrow, Katherine," Alistair's voice was gentle.

Katherine nodded as she started cleaning her eye makeup off her cheeks.

"I love you, Katherine," Alistair reassured her.

"I know," she replied, her voice soft. At least somebody did.

Katherine finished her makeup and then turned to face Alistair. She had to ask, but she was sure she already knew the answer. He wasn't asking questions, which meant he knew more than she did.

"You met and talked with my mother before she died?" Katherine tried to clear the lump from her throat.

"I did. My last night at the house, after you fell asleep, she and I had a nice visit." Alistair stood and walked toward her, towering over her so that she was forced to tilt her head up to look at him.

He was so close. She could feel his heat and smell him. She had missed him.

"You recommended your father to draw up a new will?"

He nodded. "Dora told me a story and shared a few of her fears. She knew George would do his best to keep anyone outside the family from meeting with her, and she needed help. She knew what she wanted and only needed help to make it happen."

"And you helped her?" Katherine's voice broke. She was pleased that Alistair had helped, but she was also hurt that her mother hadn't let her help.

"She didn't want you involved. She wanted you to be just as surprised as everyone else so your father couldn't use it against you," Alistair explained, reading her thoughts. "Dora was a smart woman."

"She told you about George, didn't she?" Katherine looked at Alistair's shirt buttons, unable to meet his eyes. "Was that the story she told you?"

He lifted her chin, forcing her to look at him. "She did. She admitted to being too scared to tell you. I don't believe that she knew how bad it was between you and your father, and she hoped up until the time of her death that you would never find out the truth. I think that was why she left you everything, hoping he would keep playing the doting father."

Katherine snorted. "He was never that!"

"No, but you never told her that, and neither did your father. The story she told me about your and his relationship was very different from reality.

You ended up hurting only yourself in your attempt to spare her feelings." Alistair's words were harsh, even if softly spoken, and Katherine jerked her head away from his grasp.

"So, it was my fault!" She closed her eyes at the pain of it. "Where you ever going to tell me?"

"It wasn't your fault, but a little honesty would have changed events dramatically. She hadn't been happy in her marriage for a very long time, but she stayed because she thought you and your sisters were secure." His words were like knives. "She told me to tell you if I ever thought the time was right."

"She knew I wasn't happy. She knew I wanted out, and she helped me escape!" Katherine denied that her mother thought she was completely happy. "You should have told me!"

"Dora believed that George was overprotective, which was why he wouldn't let you go. She had no idea that he was keeping you close through manipulation and guilt because of the money, and up until recently, maybe even today, I don't even think you truly believed it." Alistair followed a pacing Katherine with his eyes. "I didn't tell you because I didn't think I should be the one to do her or George's dirty work."

"She must have known why he was keeping me close to some extent because she left me everything." Katherine shook her head.

"Perhaps, but we'll never really know, will we? Maybe she's the master manipulator and smarter than the rest of us. Her sad story got me to do what she wanted." He shrugged at the thought, not particularity bothered by the fact that he may have been used.

"That doesn't bother you!" Katherine spun to look at him.

"No, because it helped you. Sure, today hurts, and it will hurt for a while, but your mother made you a powerful woman and handed you all you will ever need in one fell swoop while ensuring that you sisters will stay in your life." Alistair reached for her and pulled her against him so forcefully that all the air was pushed from her lungs.

"I know you have a lot of questions, but now we need to put this aside, and you need to join us for lunch. You need to go out there as if nothing happened." Alistair pushed her hair off her shoulder and placed his hand on her neck, feeling her pulse speeding up significantly at his touch.

"How do you propose that I do that!" she insisted, looking into his sky-blue eyes.

"By looking like you've just been kissed," he whispered against her lips before he kissed her. It was a kiss of desperation, as if he feared it would be the last.

When he broke it, Katherine looked at him with wide bewildered eyes.

"I can see you're still thinking," he said before he took her lips one more time.

This kiss did make Katherine stop thinking. It made her stop breathing as she wound her arms around his neck, pushed her hands through his hair, and started to kiss him back, pushing him up against the wall while trying to get as close to him as possible. It was the first time she had ever taken control of a kiss.

This time when they came up for air, Alistair was the one who looked at her with wide bewildered eyes. Then it was as if the clouds parted and the sun came out as he grinned down at her.

The sight made her breath hitch. "You're right. We don't have to figure this out today," she agreed as she went in for another kiss, and Alistair was all about it as he let her take charge.

However, the time came when they had to join the others, and he broke the kiss. When Katherine went to fix her makeup, he wouldn't let her as he pulled her out of the restroom and across the crowded restaurant toward a table that was already the center of attention.

"Nice," Cassie giggled as she straightened Alistair's tie when he sat next to her.

"Here, you have a little lipstick..." Laura passed him his napkin.

If Alistair looked that askew, she must look the same.

"Don't do a thing, dear. You look charming, and wear that just been kissed look better that Alistair does," Mason said as he reached over and patted her hand.

"So, Mason, how did the three of you get here so quickly?" Davis asked as the server took Alistair and Katherine's drink order.

"The restaurant rule," Mason said.

"The restaurant rule?" Wyatt asked. "I don't think that I've heard of this one." He leaned back in his chair, creating a relaxing vibe for the others to follow. He was a master at body language.

"Yes, it was created by...." Mason searched his memory for the origin.

"Bryce," Cassie provided.

Mason shrugged. "If you say so. Someone had a business meeting-"

"Bryce," Cassie said again, and Mason shot her a haughty look for interrupting.

"Fine! Bryce!" he said through clenched teeth, and the others tried to hide their smiles. He wasn't really upset, but he was playing it well.

"Bryceeeee," he drew it out, "had a business meeting, but too many of us tagged along, and no business was conducted. This frustrated my dear brother, so a rule was created that no more than four Stevens could attend any business meeting together. We knew-"

"We knew that Laura and Beth were meeting with Katherine, but we also knew that Trisha would be here with her new toy boy-" Cassie cut Mason off, eager to tell the story herself.

Katherine started choking on her drink that had been served moments earlier at hearing George described as a toy boy. "Sorry," she said between coughs.

"Which meant that something was going to go down, so we were at the restaurant two doors down just in case." Cassie finished in a rush as Beth patted Katherine on the back.

"So you already knew about my – about George?" Katherine looked at Alistair with an accusing glance.

"No, dear, we had no clue, but Trisha tends to create drama wherever she goes, and one of her favorite people to create it around is Laura." Mason waved the server over. "I'm starving."

"Why only Laura?" Katherine asked.

"Oh, it's not just me," Laura appeared to be unfazed by Trisha's trouble-making, "she's even worse when Bryce is around. She thinks we're too stodgy-"

"She thinks you were both born with sticks up your asses," Davis grinned, and Laura shot him a look that would kill a lesser man.

"She enjoys trying to embarrass them whenever possible. It's great fun." Beth giggled.

"It's only because you're not on the receiving end of it," Laura sipped her drink.

"So, you mean it works despite how cool you play it!" Alistair hooted, and the entire table erupted in laughter.

"The only one it doesn't work on is your father!" Laura shook her head with a smile, taking the teasing in stride.

"The one that got away!" Mason lifted his glass to Trisha across the restaurant, and she blew him a kiss which only made them more noticeable.

"You mean Trisha and your father were together?" Katherine asked Alistair with a frown.

"Good lord, no!" Cassie laughed. "Bryce knows Trisha too well to ever take her seriously, and she was madly in love with her husband, but she likes to tease Bryce every chance she gets that if she had ever decided to win him, he would have been hers."

Katherine snuck a look over at the table where Trisha was holding court, entertaining George and her sisters, all of whom kept sneaking glances at Katherine.

"So, going back to this restaurant rule. I'm guessing there will be no business discussed today?" Wyatt asked.

"Not with Mason around," Laura said drily as the server arrived and took their order.

The rest of the meal was spent talking about the current goings on with the family, and it was an eye-opener for Katherine. The Stevens tried to arrange their schedules so that they could spend equal time with each other whenever possible. She had known that they were close, but not that close.

Toward the end of the meal, Trisha glided over all smiles with George and Katherine's sisters in tow.

"I am assuming that a good portion of your conversation revolved around me?" she asked, eyeing everyone with her charming smile.

"You know what they say about assumptions, Trisha," Mason winked. He was talking about the saying that 'assumptions make an ass out of you and me'. It was a play on words that Katherine had only heard a few times.

"It doesn't take much to make you an ass, Mason." Trisha smiled sweetly.

"Ouch!" Mason clutched his heart.

"I came over to ensure you all will be at my barbecue and rodeo fundraiser in Virginia next month. It's for a good cause, and I need your names and your money to support the Livingston Scholarship fund." Trisha patted Davis on the shoulder. "It'll give you all a chance to rodeo. I know how much you all love that."

Katherine refused to look at George, but she smiled at her sisters, who gave her hesitant smiles in return.

"Trisha, why don't you introduce everyone?" Alistair suggested as he leaned back and placed his arm possessively across the back of Katherine's chair.

Trisha looked at the girls, eyeing Cassie and Mason eagerly, then at George, who looked like he had just sucked a lemon.

"George, Jessie, Jillian, and Jackie, this is everyone. Everyone, this is George, Jessie, Jillian, and Jackie." Trisha turned to Alistair. "How was that?"

"It was one hundred percent you, Trisha." Laura smiled.

"I have somewhere I need to be." She nodded at the table and then turned to leave, her little party following her like ducklings out of the restaurant.

"Trisha!" Mason lifted his glass, and the others followed his lead.

"I wasn't going to go to the fundraiser." Beth sighed in resignation.

"Then don't go," Katherine responded with a frown.

They all stared at her as if she had grown a second head.

"You have much to learn, my child," Mason sighed, then he clapped his hands. "Who wants dessert? Laura's buying."

It was another hour before Alistair put Katherine in a taxi with a kiss on her cheek and sent her home.

Chapter 13

Katherine's attempt to deal with the news that her entire life was a lie was slow going. It was all disturbing and upsetting, but Alistair's comment that her mother may have played them all kept her up at night.

Had she? Katherine didn't doubt that her mother loved her and her sisters, but had she played them all. If she had, why? Had it been to get even with George, or was she so alone and cut off that she felt she had no one to talk to about it all?

Katherine had tried to call her sisters several times in the past few months, but the only response she got was that their phone numbers were out of service. She wasn't sure where they were staying, so she couldn't see them in person, and they had no idea where she lived.

It had worried Katherine so much that she had called Bryce to see if he had a way to contact them, but all his office had on record was the same information Katherine had.

She eventually did have her meeting with Laura, but this time they opted for an office so that it would be productive.

There had been no word from Alistair, and Laura had mentioned that he was in London for business and wasn't sure when he would be back.

The date for Trisha's fundraiser had arrived, and Katherine wasn't particularly interested in attending. She wouldn't have if it weren't for the possibility that she would see her sisters there. As far as she knew, Trisha was still seeing George because their photos had been all over the society pages in the paper.

Laura had signed a new up-and-coming model named Armand onto her books. He was tall, dark, and handsome, with light brown eyes and a strong jaw, and he liked to look at himself a lot. Katherine wasn't impressed, but she had agreed to take him to the event so he could get some face time with the press.

The party was being held at a massive estate in Virginia, and plenty of people were already there by the time Katherine and Armand arrived. They had flown in that morning and were staying the night at a local hotel.

Armand had wide eyes as they walked through the house full of famous people. It was a fairly common occurrence for Katherine, so she hardly noticed as she kept a lookout for Alistair and her sisters.

She found her sisters first, and they were standing alone in the corner of the garden, watching people with the same awed look that Armand had. Katherine introduced him to the girls, and he was immediately smitten with Jessie.

"Can I speak with you a minute, Jessie?" Katherine asked.

Jessie smiled at Armand as she stepped to the side with her sister.

"I can't call any of you. Your numbers aren't working. What's going on?" Katherine asked, her eyes scanning the crowd.

"Dad changed our numbers without us knowing," Jessie said, crossing her arms. "I can't call any friends because I lost their numbers. It's the same for Jillian and Jackie.

It sounded like he was trying to isolate them, which was a worrying sign.

Katherine pulled out her phone. "What's your new number?" Jessie told her, and she entered it into her phone quickly. "I won't contact you unless it is an emergency." George saw them taking and was headed in their direction. "If you need me, you can always reach me through Bryce. You remember the location of his office?"

Jessie nodded. "I have a lot of questions."

"So do I. Maybe we can figure out the answers together." Katherine gave her a wobbly smile.

"Girls, come with me, the rodeo is about to start, and we don't want to miss any of the action," George said as he grabbed Jessie by the arm and pulled her away from Katherine.

Armand joined Katherine where she stood watching George.

"Who's the old man?" he asked with a frown.

"He's Jessie's father." It felt odd not calling him her father.

Armand held out his arm for Katherine. "Should we join the others?"

Everyone was headed down a steep hill toward what looked to be a quickly erected corral with steel barricades. In the middle of it were some cowboys and horses.

Katherine saw the Stevens clan on the other side of the corral but didn't feel comfortable enough with them to join them without an invitation.

Alistair was there with a beautiful redhead she didn't recognize hanging off his arm, and Katherine felt her heart clench at the sight.

Beth saw her and waved, and Katherine waved back as she did her best to keep her eyes from straying to Alistair.

The men in the corral started the show. There was roping and riding, some barrel racing, and a tired-looking bull who put up a half-hearted fight when the cowboy rode him. Katherine couldn't take it any longer and looked across the corral again, only to have Laura beckon them in her direction.

Laura and Armand joined the Stevens group, who all looked bored with the rodeo.

"I would have thought this would have been more interesting for your family," Katherine commented as she looked at the Stevens, who were all having conversations or on their phones.

"According to Davis, these guys aren't the real deal." Laura shrugged. "With a few rodeo champs in the family, they should know."

"Maybe they should get out there and show them the ropes!" Armand smiled at his pun.

"They are all in their 60s. They would probably break something. The only ones who could do it would be the kids." Cassie said as she joined them, hugging Katherine while eyeing Armand.

"Cassie, this is Armand, Armand, this is Cassie Stevens." Katherine introduced. She's Laura's sister-in-law." Armand took Cassie's hand and kissed it.

"Does Armand have a last name?" Mason asked, looking at him over Cassie's shoulder. He looked jealous, and the thought amused Katherine.

"No, just Armand," Katherine said as he watched Armand smile widely at the famous couple.

The redhead who had her arm through Alistair's wandered over to them and smiled at Katherine.

Mason coughed something that sounded like the word lazy and wandered off again.

"Alistair's mood has changed, and now he's all sullen," the woman said as she eyed Katherine.

"Katherine, this is my oldest daughter, Aggie. I don't think you've ever met before," Cassie introduced. "She's married to Trisha's nephew."

Katherine felt relief flood through her at the fact that she was Alistair's cousin. She hadn't noticed before, but the woman was pregnant. "We met once, years ago, but I didn't recognize you."

"I don't recall either. You're Alistair's Katherine?" Aggie asked, eyeing Katherine with interest. Her eyes moved to Armand with a dawning realization. "Well, that explains it."

Katherine blushed at being called Alistair's Katherine.

"Explains what?" Davis asked, joining them and looking into his camera with a frown. "I can't get any good shots. "I wonder if Mason and Alistair would be willing to get in there and do a little cutting?"

"Cutting?" Kathrine asked, only because it involved Alistair.

"Cutting cattle, dear," Trisha said as she joined Davis looking over his shoulder.

"There are not enough cattle," Aggie said. "Katherine's Armand explains why Alistair's in a sudden bad mood." Katherine was learning that it wasn't uncommon for the Stevenses to have multiple conversations going at once.

Davis looked at Laura. "You didn't tell him?"

Laura shrugged. "Should I have?"

"Tell him what?" Cassie asked, confused.

"Laura asked Katherine to bring Armand for the press. It's the oldest trick in the book to get new talent noticed." Davis frowned again, then wandered off with Trisha on his heels.

Cassie and Aggie both looked over at Laura with knowing grins.

"There's hope for you yet," Cassie squealed as she hugged Laura.

Had Laura not mentioned it on purpose to make Alistair jealous? Were they really that much on Katherine's side?

Laura took it in stride, but Katherine swore she was trying not to smile. "I usually don't tell Alistair about my business decisions," Laura defended herself, but it was half-hearted at best.

"Cassie, did you pack my jeans and boots?" Mason asked, rubbing his hands together as he appeared from nowhere.

"Are we at a rodeo?" Mason missed the sarcasm in her voice as he kissed her.

"What about Alistair?" Aggie called, but Mason only waved his hand as if it was a technicality.

"It was only a matter of time, I suppose," Laura smiled. "Davis will do anything for the shot."

"Here's hoping Mason doesn't break something." Cassie shook her head at the thought.

Katherine knew she was missing something but wasn't sure what it was.

"They're only the top picks because Caleb and Quinn aren't here," Laura added.

"Or Fiona and Henry," Aggie chipped into the conversation.

Half an hour later, Mason entered the corral, holding up his hand in greeting as everyone went crazy when they realized who it was. Katherine watched as Alistair entered the corral behind him more subtly.

Katherine's breath caught as she looked at him. Someone had found him the proper clothing, and he wore it like a second skin. His jeans were tight, and his hat was pulled low, shielding his eyes.

Aggie and Cassie snorted their disbelief as the trained cowboys tried to give Mason and Alistair a quick lesson with the horse and rope.

"Who's taking them to the hospital if one of them does break something?" Laura asked through thinned lips.

Cassie and Aggie looked at each other and then did a quick rock paper scissors to decide. Aggie won or lost. Katherine wasn't sure which, but either way, she couldn't take her eyes off Alistair.

There were catcalls from the ladies in the audience, and Katherine frowned. Now she was jealous.

When the cowboy stepped aside, Mason and Alistair met in the center of the corral, where they talked about something before they each moved to their separate horses.

Katherine looked on in fascination as they each spent a few minutes with their assigned horses, and Alistair looked as natural with his horse as he did in a tux at a concert.

A few more calves were released on the other side of the corral, where they stayed bunched together.

Mason grabbed the rope off the side of the saddle and ran it through his hands as Alistair easily mounted his horse in one fluid motion. Kathrine noticed that he had gloves on his hands where they flexed on the horse's reins.

A hush descended on the crowd, and Mason said something that made Alistair laugh.

"You can take the man out of Texas, but you can't take Texas out of the man," Cassie sighed, her eyes glued to Mason. "I love watching him on a horse."

Katherine looked over at Alistair and got it. The way Alistair was efficiently controlling the horse with one hand while his muscles flexed in reaction to the horse's movements. It was poetry.

Mason mounted and looked at Alistair before giving a sharp whistle.

Then they were off. Mason had the rope out in a flash and roped a calf on his first try. Alistair was quick off his saddle as he grabbed the calf, dropped it, and tied it. It was over in a minute, and the crowd went wild.

Mason waved to everyone as Alistair untied the calf and then gathered the rope with a grin.

"Uh-oh, I know that look," Aggie whispered as Mason dismounted and started to coil his rope.

Before everyone knew what happened, Alistair had his rope out and it raced through the air to lasso his uncle.

Mason reached up and pushed his hat up, then grinned at his nephew as he dragged his uncle across the corral and handed the rope to Cassie.

Cassie climbed up on the barrier and dropped a big kiss on Mason's lips.

Realizing that the show was over, the crowd started to wander back up to the house, but Katherine was still staring at Alistair, realizing that she knew nothing about him because it had always been about her.

Chapter 14

Katherine stood watching Alistair as he talked with the cowboys. He appeared to fit right in with them as if they had been friends for years instead of having just met. Everyone but a few hangers-on, who not surprisingly were women, had drifted back up to the house, and Armand was eager to join them.

"Katherine, should we go up to the house now?" Armand asked impatiently.

"You go ahead. Maybe I'll catch up with you later, but if not, don't worry about it," Katherine said absentmindedly, her eyes glued to Alistair.

"Sounds good!" Armand said, sounding pleased to be left to his own devices.

Katherine moved to the shade of a tree and sunk onto a grassy spot of earth as she watched Alistair spend some time with the horse he had ridden before helping the cowboys begin the process of packing up.

Some of the women gave up and wandered away, but eventually, some of the braver ones approached Alistair with a smile and swaying hips. A few slips of paper were handed to him, which Katherine guessed to be phone numbers, and Alistair pocketed them all with his signature grin before tipping the brim of his hat to them.

It was all so effortless for him. He didn't even have to try.

She felt all her old insecurities building up, and instead of pushing them back as she always did, she let them come. What was her real fear? Was it that she wasn't good enough for him?

She knew in her mind that she was, but her heart doubted. She was a model with a television career and enough of her own money never to need his. His family thought she was good enough for him because they kept pushing them together.

Was it the fact that he was part of the English aristocracy? No, it wasn't on her wish list to carry a title, but she had become accustomed to attending formal events and socializing with strangers. Katherine thought of the story Alistair had told her about his mother. She understood why he had told her the story, it was to prove that she was as capable as his mother of carrying the title, and she probably was in the end.

So what was it?

Katherine watched another girl tuck her hair behind her ear and bat her eyelashes at Alistair's grinning face, and it dawned on her. She was afraid that he would get bored with her. Once he caught her, he would no longer want her because the chase would be over. It had happened with George and her mother.

George had never bothered to hide the fact that Dora bored him. She couldn't handle it if all of Alistair's desire and love for her dried up to boredom. It would be worse than a death sentence because she knew she would never grow bored with him. She could watch him for hours.

She didn't think he would become cruel with boredom, but Dora probably never believed George would be cruel.

It all boiled down to one thing, she didn't know or understand him, not really. Other than a few days a few times a year, they had never spent much time together.

Katherine had stopped looking at Alistair as her thoughts turned inward, and she started to recall all the little mean things George had done to Dora. He had always ignored her at parties or made her the punch line of a joke. He never remembered her birthday or celebrated any special occasion with her, and he had been the same with Katherine.

"My new friends think you're too shy to come over and introduce yourself to me," Alistair said as he lowered himself onto the ground next to her and leaned back on his elbows, his long, lean legs clad in tight denim stretched in front of him.

Katherine gave a weak smile. "Maybe a little," she agreed, which caused Alistair to look up at her from under the brim of his hat with a frown.

"Who is the guy with you?" he asked as he looked back toward the corral.

"Are you jealous," Katherine smiled slightly at the ridiculous thought.

"Yes, very," he admitted, focusing on the corral.

"Are you really?" she asked in disbelief, hugging her knees to her chest. It was hard for her to believe.

"It's not something I would lie about, Katherine." His blue eyes met hers, and she melted a little.

"I'm jealous of all the phone numbers you just pocketed. It looked as if there were half a dozen," Katherine looked at her bare toes in their sandals.

"Who's the guy, Katherine," he growled.

"Didn't I say?" she teased, enjoying the fact that he was jealous.

"Are you two dating? Is he your boyfriend?" he demanded.

"Boyfriend." She rolled the word around in her head. "I've never had a boyfriend," Katherine admitted to herself.

"Then what was I?" Alistair asked, looking at her through narrowed eyes.

"A lover, my first and only," she whispered. She laid her cheek on her knees and watched him absorb that.

"How did I not know that!" he sat up and turned toward her with wide eyes.

"I'm good at pretending to know what I'm doing when really I don't. It's my life story. Plus, it was natural and right with you, but I don't think of you as my lover past tense, Alistair." She closed her eyes. "Is that how you see us?"

"No!" he reached for her but dropped his hand at the last minute.

"I still don't understand. There are physical signs." He shook his head.

"I did gymnastics and rode horses. Who knows, it's not unheard of for the physical markers to be erased through childhood endeavors." Katherine swallowed a lump in her throat as she opened her eyes and looked at him. "Do you not believe me?"

"I didn't say that." He shook his head as he looked at the house with a frown.

"I didn't know you could rope or ride so well." She heard the catch in her throat, and she cleared it.

"Katherine, I didn't say I don't believe you." This time when he reached for her, he grabbed her hand, picking up on the fact that she was upset.

"No, you didn't say it, did you." Perhaps they were past tense. Somehow, she felt that the Alistair of old would have believed her without hesitation. Something had changed, but she wasn't sure what it was. "What's changed? There was a time you would never have doubted it," Katherine forced herself to ask the hard question.

"I received a call from your production company last week. They want to film at the house." Alistair stood and crossed his arms.

"They mentioned it at our production meeting last time I was in London." Katherine nodded, confused as to why it was a problem.

"We had this out years ago. I don't want you to film at the house." His voice was tight.

"Then say no, Alistair. It doesn't make a difference to me. In fact, I told them you probably wouldn't allow it." Katherine stood as well, brushing off her skirt.

"It's just convenient, that's all." Alistair turned to walk away from her, but she wasn't going to let him. She felt that the very thing she had just discovered she feared the most was about to happen. Alistair was going to be cruel.

"What's convenient?" It was barely a whisper, but he heard it.

"You suddenly decide to tell me that you gave me your innocence only a week after your production crew asks to film in a house that we have never allowed anyone to film in before." Alistair crossed his arms defensively, and his jaw was tight in displeasure. "Either that or you didn't expect me to be here, and you're trying to distract me from the fact that you brought another, what? Lover? Or did you bring him to make me jealous?"

Katherine had never seen him so cold before, and she felt her heart shattering in her chest. "His name is Armand, he is one of Laura's clients, and she asked me to bring him so that he could get some press and start meeting the right people," she whispered, then took deep, measured breaths as she tried to calm herself, turning her attention toward the men in the corral. "I told you about being a virgin to reassure you that you've been the only man in my life not to get a production deal." She forced herself to meet his eyes. "I was waiting here to apologize to you."

"Apologize, so it's true?" his eyes grew wide.

"No, Alistair, it's not, and I just told you that you're off base. I wanted to apologize because I realize that I have never taken the time to get to know who you are, and that has made me unsure of you. I realized it today when I saw you roping." She took a deep breath. "I pushed you away because I feared that you would decide, once we were in a full-time relationship, that you wouldn't want me. That you would be as cruel to me as George was to my mother when you realized that fact."

Alistair's expression didn't alter as he watched the emotions chase across Katherine's face.

"But it's clear that you never fully knew me, either, and now you don't want to so you're pushing me away with cruel words. Goodbye, Alistair." Katherine couldn't hold back the tears any longer and turned and fled.

His words of love had meant nothing in the end. Just as she was sure, George's words of love meant nothing to her mother.

******

Alistair didn't know how long he stood under that tree watching the rodeo cleanup, but they were long gone by the time he made a move.

He had just made the biggest mistake of his life. How had he not realized she was innocent all those years ago? Why had she never shared that with him? Part of his overreaction was anger that he hadn't realized it.

Alistair was hurt when he got the call about the production company wanting to use the house. He thought that was all over long ago. But why didn't she come to him herself if it was still something she wanted? Why did she have the production crew do it? He was already sensitive about Katherine, and a man could only take so many rejections before he began to believe it was all a game.

It would be like someone playing games to claim innocence when they needed a leg up in the game. The fact that she had teased him about the man she was with and it was a side of her he had never seen before. It could have been her coming out of her shell and gaining some confidence, but it also could have been her evading the truth or slipping up.

It would also be like a woman playing games to bring a date to make him jealous, and he was mad that it had worked. He had flirted a little more than he usually would with the women who approached him, attempting to make her jealous, too.

Didn't that make him the one that was playing games?

Alistair was turned inside out and was all twisted up inside. One thing he was sure of was that he had hurt her in the way she had feared he would, which meant she was in the wind. She wouldn't reach out to him again, so he would have to bring her to him.

He would have to let the production company into the house. It was the only way.

Chapter 15

Two weeks later, Katherine had just finished washing the dishes from her quickly prepared dinner that she had to force herself to eat when there was a knock on the door. Not many people knew her address, so she couldn't imagine who it might be. She wiped her hands on a towel and moved to the door to look through the peephole.

She was surprised to see all three of her sisters standing on the other side.

Katherine opened the door and held it wide for them to enter without saying a word as they entered the small space, looking around curiously.

The apartment had belonged to Beth when Katherine had moved in nine years earlier. When Beth and Wyatt had married, Beth sold the apartment to her. It was two bedrooms, one bathroom, and a kitchen-living room combo. It was dated, but since Katherine wasn't there much, it suited her needs.

"I expected something grander?" Jackie said as she sat down on the couch with a bounce.

"I don't need much, and I don't spend that much time here." Katherine perched on a chair, watching Jillian and Jessie as they poked around. It was rude, but they were her little sisters, so she was used to it.

"Bryce gave us your address like you said he would," Jessie said, sitting on the couch next to her sister, taking stock of Katherine as if she was seeing her in a new light. "I was curious how you knew all those famous people, so I did a little digging."

"We had no clue that you were a model and had your own television show in England, Katie!" Jillian exclaimed as she sat in the other chair across from Katherine. "Why did you keep it from us?"

"I didn't do it purposely. We just never had much to do with each other after I left. I told Mom, and I thought she would have told you." Katherine shrugged.

"No, she wouldn't have. She wouldn't have wanted George to know," Jessie softly said.

"George?" Katherine asked, looking at her sister. "Don't tell me you're his step-children too?" Katherine wouldn't be surprised by anything regarding George.

"No, he's our father," Jessie grimaced, "but we decided if you have to call him George, we should too."

Katherine felt tears threatening, and she cleared her throat. "You know that it's not necessary, right? I don't want to ever come between you and George." It meant the world to her that they would stand up for her like that. She had never expected it.

"It was as much a surprise to us as it was to you," Jillian said with a sad expression. "Why wouldn't Mom tell you or us about something like that?"

"I wish I knew. I also wish I knew my real father and what happened to him." Katherine stared vacantly at the pattern in the carpet as she thought about it.

"Well, no matter what, we're your sisters," Jackie said with an assertiveness that made Katherine smile.

"And I'm grateful for it. I'm also glad that you decided to come to visit me." Katherine leaned back in her chair.

"We want to do more than a visit," Jillian said, biting her lip as she looked at the other two sisters. "We are all legal adults now and don't want to be under George's thumb anymore. We thought we could crash here until we figure out what we want to do."

Katherine sat up in her chair again as she looked at the three of them, who looked so hopeful that she would say yes. "I travel a lot. Would you all be all right here on your own without me?"

The only reason Katherine could think of for them not to live with her was that it would change her life dramatically, but would that be a bad thing? She had lost Alistair and was looking at a lifetime of loneliness stretched out before her. Having a close connection with her sisters might keep her sane.

"Maybe we could travel with you sometimes?" Jackie shyly suggested.

"We would be fine on our own!" Jillian shot Jackie a warning look. They had a plan and didn't want to ask for too much too quickly. "George isn't around much anyway. He travels a lot or is out with Trisha."

"I don't suppose any of you know how serious it is with Trisha?" Katherine asked worriedly as she thought of George pulling a fast one on Trisha.

"I think she's toying with him," Jessie said with a frown. "I like her, and if she were to marry George, living with him might be bearable, but I think her only interest in him is sex."

Katherine was so shocked at her sister's words that she gasped, but it was too quick, and she started to cough.

"How do you know her?" Jillian asked, looking at her coughing sister.

"We share friends," Katherine took a deep breath attempting to steady her voice.

"Alistair?" Jessie asked, watching her. "How long have you known him?"

"Are you jealous, Jessie?" Jackie giggled.

"No, but I think it's serious between them, and I'm curious if he's going to be our brother-in-law." Jessie stared Katherine down and watched as she blushed. "You would gain a heck of a family if you did marry him?"

"You're my family," Katherine assured her and watched some tension leave Jessie's shoulders. "Alistair and I have known each other for a long time, but we've had a falling out and are no longer talking." She couldn't hide her sadness as she said it.

"Maybe you will make up soon," Jillian said hopefully.

"Maybe," Katherine's tone was half-hearted at best as she forced a smile.

"So, about us staying here?" Jillian asked, moving on as the young often do when thinking about themselves.

"And us traveling with you?" Jackie grinned.

"You can stay here, but it will be a squeeze. You can travel with me when I go to London if you like since I have an apartment there-"

"You do!" Jackie squeaked as she bounced once on the sofa.

"But for my modeling trips, you will have to stay here. Those are work-related, and I'm only ever there for a few days at most." Katherine had to raise her voice as they started to squeal in excitement.

"What about school?" she looked at Jillian and Jackie.

"Would you be mad if we didn't return to school immediately?" Jackie asked. Katherine was quickly learning that she was the bravest in the group.

"It's your life. I would advise that if you decide not to do that, you at least have a plan. I'm not going to be stingy with your allowance, but I would like to see you each earning a living and making your way in the world." Katherine looked at each of her sisters, hoping they got the point.

"George only wanted us to marry well." Jillian thought out loud as if nothing else had ever occurred to her.

"He wanted to use us as bargaining tools." Jessie shook her head. "Is that what he wanted for you, Katie?"

"No." Katherine shook her head as she thought of all the mean things he had said to her in her youth. She didn't want to tell them the truth because she didn't want to color their judgment of their father. If she did, that would make her as bad as he was.

"He wasn't very nice to you or Mom. I heard him going off on you once when he didn't think anyone was around." Jessie said, watching Katherine closely.

"Why did he do that?" Jackie asked, looking at Katherine, who only shrugged in response.

"He wanted to control Mom's money and did it through Katherine. I don't know what kind of deal he and Mom made, but you and your paternity were a part of it." Jessie was not shy about throwing George under the bus.

"Is that what you think, Katie?" Jillian asked.

"Yes." Katherine's voice broke. "But no more of that? Where are your things?"

Jackie jumped up. "They're at the house. George's out of town this week, so we thought it would be a good time to make a move."

Jessie's phone dinged as if on cue, and she looked at it with a frown. "It will have to wait. He's home. His flight was canceled, and he wants to know where we are."

The girls' faces fell, and they looked distraught at the prospect. They had to get him out of the house now, while they all had the courage to make the move and before he found out what was going on. Katherine's mind quickly jumped from idea to idea before she landed on Trisha.

"Tell him you're having a late lunch and seeing a movie," Katherine said as she reached for her phone. She texted Laura and asked her for Trisha's number. The best thing about Laura was that she wasn't overly curious, and Katherine had the number in less than five minutes.

"Are you sure you want to do this?" Katherine looked at them once more. "I have a plan to get you out tonight if you're sure." It was a test. If they said yes and didn't hesitate, they were sure, but if they hesitated, they should probably go back to George.

"We're sure, but will it be worth it if he finds us?" Jessie worried.

"He won't find you. He doesn't know where I live." Katherine dialed Trisha's number.

"Won't Bryce tell him?" Jillian asked with a frown.

"Not unless I tell him to."

Trisha answered on the third ring.

"Trisha, this is Katherine." Katherine knew she was going out on a limb trusting Trisha, but the Stevens family did, which was good enough for her.

"Alistair's Katherine?" Katherine could hear the mischievous smile in her voice as if she knew her words had made Katherine blush.

"Yes. The girls want to run away from home. Could you help me get them away from George tonight?" Jackie and Jillian looked at each other nervously as Katherine spoke.

"George wants us home now!" Jessie hissed.

"Hmmm, for good, or will they go back?" She sounded as if she had all the time in the world.

"For good, they're going to live with me for a while," Katherine admitted believing honesty was the best policy.

"Oh, that sounds nice, dear. Shall I ask him out for a leisurely dinner?" Trisha suggested.

"That would be perfect." Katherine agreed.

"Yes, it would be. I'll get him out of the house and send the car back for the girls. If you put them in a taxi, he can trace them. I take it he doesn't know where you live, which is the point of the secrecy?" Trisha muttered something that Katherine couldn't hear to someone with her.

"Yes, the girls found me through Bryce," Katherine explained, wondering why Trisha was so good at covert thinking.

"Bryce," Trisha sighed. "What might have been? You're lucky to get his son."

Katherine didn't correct her. She only muttered something that didn't make much sense.

"No matter," Trisha said. "I'll clear the way for you." Then Trisha ended the call abruptly.

"Trisha's going to help us?" Jillian said with surprise.

"Yes, but now you must go home and act as if nothing is wrong. She'll send a car for you once they're at dinner."

The girls nodded as Katherine told them to take the subway, not a Taxi.

As she watched them go, she felt that her life would never be the same. Since she couldn't be part of the Stevens family, maybe she could create the same closeness with her own. It was a novel thought and one she never thought she would have.

Chapter 16

The girls had been living with Katherine for three months, and so far, it had worked well. They were each developing interests of their own, and none of them were lying about the apartment and getting in the way while doing nothing, which Katherine had feared would happen when they moved into with her.

Katherine had concluded that they had wanted to be adults for a while, but their father had kept them under his thumb the same as he had with Katherine ten years before.

Now, they were in London because Katherine was about to start filming for the television show she hosted, and she would be traveling around Britain for at least four months as she shot the series. When she had suggested that the girls come and stay with her in London, they had been eager to join her.

They had also been eager to join her at the black-tie event that they were currently attending. Katherine had told them no at first, but when Laura told her that she was to be part of the "rent a famous date for the evening" portion of the program, Katherine had changed her mind and insisted that they attend with her for moral support.

Laura had agreed to have Katherine attend and participate in the fundraiser during her contract renewal with the production company, which left Katherine where she was now, all decked out in her cream ball gown with her hair in an up-do that had taken the hairstylist two hours to accomplish waiting for the bidding to begin. All anyone in her social circle had talked about for the last week was this event, and by the looks of the crowd, it was the place to see and be seen.

"Katherine," Grace said from behind Katherine, where she sat at the round table with her sisters and a few other guests.

"Grace," she said as she stood and placed her cheek against Grace's in the familiar greeting as her eyes darted around the room. If Grace was attending, then Bryce would be as well, and there was also a high probability that Alistair would be attending too.

Katherine felt her heart stop and then start beating erratically at the thought. Despite his accusations months earlier, she still missed Alistair, and she still wanted him. However, she knew he didn't want anything to do with her, so a meeting of any kind would be awkward because he would see her need.

Katherine had just finished introducing Grace to her sisters when Bryce joined them, handing Grace a drink as he greeted all four girls with his usual vague expression as his eyes scanned the room.

"I saw that you were on the auction list. Your date looks intriguing." Grace said as she opened the brochure to reread it. It says an "All American Girl home-cooked meal." That sounds nice. Although I don't know what cooking has to do with the American Girl part."

"I haven't quite figured it out either. Perhaps it has to do with the food that is cooked?" Katherine thought aloud. She hadn't had a say in the description, so she hoped that whoever, if anyone did, bid on her package was forgiving. The entire thing was out of her comfort zone. She was scared to death that no one would bid at all.

"Are you a good cook?" Grace asked with a smile.

"No! I can only cook a few things, and none are particularly American." Katherine could hear the panic in her voice and took a deep breath, forcing herself to calm down.

"It's for a good cause, and you're brave to do this," Grace said, placing her hand on Katherine's arm. "I'll tell you what. Bryce and I promise to place a bid on your package if no one else does. How's that?"

Katherine could only smile her thanks and nod.

"Did you hear that, Bryce?" Grace said over her shoulder.

"Yes," was his droll reply.

A call went out for all those who were part of the auction to please meet behind the stage at the far end of the ballroom.

"Good luck, dear!" Grace said as she and Bryce moved to take their seats.

"You're going to do well. I can feel it!" Jackie said with a grin.

"But if not, we'll get something nice and fattening for dessert afterward." Jillian grinned as well.

Katherine turned and moved toward the stage and looked at all the familiar faces about to join her in this humiliating experience. There were a few news anchors, an actor or two, an artist, and an author, to name a few.

She was about midway down the bidding list, which was a decent place to be. She didn't want to go first because who does, and she didn't want to go at the end in case everyone had already spent their money, and she was the only alternative.

At least she would have one bid, thanks to Grace and Bryce, and that was something.

She watched as each person seemed to be happy with the result of their bid, and as the audience warmed up, it turned into a heated competition. When it was Katherine's turn she connected with her professional persona, which allowed her to joke with the Master of Ceremonies, smile for the crowd, and preen as the bids flew. The numbers were inching up when an outrageous amount was shouted from the back of the room. Katherine could barely hear the bidder and was amazed that the Master of Ceremonies had.

The gavel came down on an astonishing amount.

"An All-American Girl home-cooked meal goes to the young Earl of Pennington. Congratulations, sir!" The Master of Ceremonies said with a smile.

Katherine waved to the crowd with a smile even though her heart was pounding at the fact that Alistair had just bid on and won a date with her.

Why would he do that after what had happened the last time he had seen her?

Katherine made her way back to her table, where her sisters fell on her with congratulations.

"Oh my God, you had an earl bid on your date!" Jackie said excitedly. "Maybe you two will fall madly in love and get married!"

"Maybe we will at that," Alistair said as he sat in an empty chair next to Katherine.

Katherine smiled tightly at Alistair. "Congratulations, your grace."

"Your grace?" Jillian asked.

"Yes, Alistair is the young Earl Pennington. His father, Bryce Stevens, is still the current earl." Katherine explained.

"Our lawyer is an earl!" Jillian's eyes grew wide at the thought.

Jessie was looking from one to the other as she finally made the determination that something was going on between Katherine and Alistair.

"Do you have a moment to settle a time and place for our All-American experience?" Alistair asked, ignoring her sisters' stares.

Katherine hadn't met his eyes, and she nodded without looking at him as he waited for her to join him.

"I'll be back shortly," she told her sisters before she followed Alistair's straight back out of the hotel's ballroom.

It felt like she was being led to the firing squad. He had made his feelings toward her very clear the last time they had met, so why was he doing this now?

She was about to find out one way or another because she would not be honoring the bid unless he told her.

Chapter 17

K atherine followed Alistair out of the hotel lobby and onto the street.

"Why are we out here?" Katherine asked, rubbing her arms. It was fall, and the weather was turning colder. She hadn't anticipated spending much time outside, so her dress was sleeveless.

Alistair pulled her off to the side of the building and took off his jacket, draping it over her shoulders. It enveloped Katherine in his smell and warmth, and she couldn't help the deep breath she took, inhaling his scent.

"Being in a hotel lobby with you is too tempting, and I don't want the distraction while we talk, especially looking as beautiful as you do now." Alistair rubbed her arms to warm her up. "I'm sorry, Katherine" He came directly to the point.

Katherine took a moment to take in his blue eyes and cleanly shaven jaw, noticing that his hair was longer than usual and it curled temptingly around his collar. She liked it when it grew a little long. It was easier to run her fingers through.

She gave herself a mental shake and tried to recall the accusations he had thrown at her the last time they met.

"You need a haircut!" she exclaimed. He didn't, but she felt a criticism might keep her grounded and make it appear that she was apathetic to his apology at best.

He smiled, which was not the result she had intended.

"Why are you sorry, and is that why you bid on my package?" She crossed her arms and gave her most stern expression.

His grin grew. "It's a good thing Uncle Mason or my cousin Agatha aren't here right now. They could do so much with that statement."

"Alistair!" she warned.

"I'm sorry I accused you of having another lover, bringing another man to make me jealous, and using your innocence to get me to agree to film at my house. I know none of those things are true." His voice was low and urgent.

"The lover and jealous part I get and can forgive, and it's a little more than me using my innocence to get you to agree to the house. It's the fact that you didn't believe me! What have I ever lied to you about!" She heard her voice rising and took a deep breath, forcing herself to calm down. "Let's go back and look at the angle you just used, that I was using my innocence. The last time you proposed, I told you I wouldn't use you in any way. If I were a user, I definitely would have used you then!" She felt the tears of frustration building.

"Fine, Katherine! If you want to get mad, then I can get mad too!" He crossed his arms. "I was jealous. I have never seen you with another man in a social setting, and yes, it upset me, but that's not the worst. The worst is that you always tell me, no, and it's always for a different reason! Forgive me if I do feel used. I love you, and I made that point very clear early on, but it was never enough!"

"You will never get it because you come from a loving family!" Katherine shook her head. "The only love I have ever known is motherly love. I never even saw love between my parents, so forgive me if I don't trust you or myself when it comes to love. I am only starting to learn about sisterly love because my father did his best to keep us separated our whole lives, which I am beginning to discover was another way to isolate me."

Alistair's phone started a constant dinging, but to his credit, he ignored it as he listened to her.

"Why did you bid on me? Was it so we could have this conversation, which is going nowhere?"

"Yes, I wanted to talk to you and get you to forgive me, and I didn't want anyone else to win you." His phone was still going crazy.

"Maybe you should check that?" Katherine said.

"Not until you agree that I was stupid and promise to think about forgiving me!" He reached for her arms again and pulled her close.

Katherine caved and let him pull her against him.

"I can be stupid sometimes. I was also mad at myself that I didn't realize that you were so innocent the first time we made love. It was a chance that I lost. If I had known, maybe I could have made it more special or something!" His eyes looked longingly into hers. "It wasn't fair that you kept that experience from me."

Katherine felt tears building. "I'm sorry. I never thought of it that way. I was embarrassed that I was still a virgin. I didn't want you to know for fear that you might change your mind or think differently of me."

"Katherine, I wanted you from the moment I met you, and nothing could ever change that. You're my weakness. My pride should have kicked in when I thought you had another lover, but it didn't. All I could think of was getting you away from him."

"But it kicked in when you thought I was lying about my innocence," she pointed out in a soft voice.

"Of course, it did! My mind immediately thought about if I was good enough our first time. If I had taken my time and done it right." He sounded angry again, and it made Katherine laugh.

"If you hadn't done it right, there never would have been a second time," she reassured him.

"Do you forgive me?" he asked.

"I do, but it doesn't solve the bigger problem." Katherine took off her jacket and handed it back to him, preparing to end the conversation.

"What's the bigger problem, Katherine? Tell me so I can fix it, and we can get on with it. I miss you." He took his jacket and draped it over his arm as his phone started again.

"You had better deal with that," Katherine said, realizing it was important.

"Not until you tell me the bigger problem," he insisted.

"There you are!" Bryce said as he exited the hotel behind them as a car pulled up to the curb. "We have to go now!"

Grace followed behind him with tears streaming down her cheeks as she typed a message on her phone.

"Oh, Alistair!" Grace cried when she saw him. "It's Mave! She's been attacked!"

"Attacked?" Alistair asked with a frown.

"She was kidnapped, held at knife point, and attacked by a crazed fan!" Grace reached out and pulled her son close in a hug.

Bryce opened the car door and helped his wife into the car before following her. "Make your goodbyes quick. The plane is waiting," he said before he closed the door to give them some privacy.

Katherine looked at Alistair, who had gone very pale, and went up on tiptoe, placing a quick kiss on his cheek. "I love you, go." She whispered as she held him tight against her for a moment.

Alistair looked shell-shocked as he nodded and walked toward the car when she released him.

"I'll see you soon?" he asked, looking over his shoulder.

"Sure," she agreed with a sad smile that wasn't very convincing. "I still owe you a home-cooked meal." It seemed to be what he wanted to hear because he nodded and climbed into the car.

Katherine watched it drive away, hoping that Mave was all right. Unlike Katherine, she was a natural fighter, so she would be fine, especially with her family to back her up.

Suddenly feeling the chill, she turned and returned to the hotel to rejoin her sisters.

****

Alistair pulled out his phone and started scrolling through the missed messages. It wasn't pretty. Mave was in the intensive care unit at a hospital in Los Angeles. Nothing was clear except that she had been taken, attacked, and somehow had gotten away.

"Did you and Katherine work everything out?" Grace asked, looking over at her son with worried concern.

"Not really. I need a plan and her and we need to be together in one place for longer than a day." He frowned at what he was reading.

"You could let them film at the house," Grace suggested. They knew she was trying to change the subject to keep from thinking the worst, and Alistair and Bryce were willing to play along.

"Would you and Dad be all right with that?" Alistair asked, looking at his father, who was typing into his phone.

"With the right contract, yes," he agreed.

It was always about the deal with his father.

"Oh!" Grace cried, unable to hold back the tears any longer, "what if Mave's not all right!"

Bryce pulled her close, unable to speak.

"Then we'll deal with it as a family like we always do," Alistair said, finally understanding what Katherine had meant. She was all alone and had been most of her life. She didn't know how not to be. It was something that he and his family took for granted.

"Mom, can I ask you something?" Alistair asked when she had calmed a bit.

"Yes, love." Grace nodded.

"Was it hard to accept or understand that you were part of a close family and weren't alone anymore when you married Dad?"

"Maybe a little, but your grandmother was there, pulling me in, making me feel loved, wanted, and included. Her acceptance and warmth surrounded me, and that helped." Grace lifted her head from Bryce's shoulder.

"Is that what is going on with Katherine?" she asked, intrigued.

"Yes, she had a rotten childhood and doesn't know how to be..." he shook his head, unable to explain.

"She doesn't know how to let herself be accepted and loved for who she is, not whom she thinks she should be." Grace understood better than he had hoped.

"I think this calls for a family intervention." Grace nodded, then thought of Mave and started to cry again. "It will have to wait, though."

"It's waited nine years. It can wait a little longer," Alistair admitted.

"Nine years!" Grace exclaimed. "My poor boy!" she reached out and touched his cheek. "Poor Katherine. To deny herself love for that long. We'll fix it," she promised.

Bryce lifted his head from his phone and looked at his son. "You're in it now."

Their phones all went off simultaneously, and that ended the conversation.

They were rushing Mave into surgery for internal bleeding.

Chapter 18

- -

Katherine had done her best to keep up with Mave's status, but it had been hard. A brief mention of the attack gave almost no details in the press before the story disappeared from all forms of media. Nearly three months later, it was as if it had never happened. She had spoken to Laura briefly about how successful her appearance at the charity benefit had been and that it would stand her in good stead with her audience, but when she asked after Mave, Laura hadn't shared any details other than she was on the mend.

It was frustrating because Katherine did care, but it reminded her that while the Stevenses were kind to her, she wasn't family or even a friend, only an acquaintance.

Katherine was riding in the back of the crew van, looking at her phone, when she heard a low whistle from the front.

"This is definitely the grandest house we've ever investigated!" J.D, the cameraman, exclaimed. "It will be a joy to shoot. I bet there isn't a bad angle in the house."

Robert, who was driving the van, stopped halfway up the drive, and they all craned their necks to get a view of the house. However, it wasn't enough for some, as the door to the van was opened, and they all spilled out, taking photos of the dramatic setting.

"It's like a movie set," Claire, the makeup artist and hairstylist, said in awe as she snapped a selfie.

"It is lovely," Kiki agreed.

"Where are we?" Katherine asked with a frown. She had been traveling the last month and didn't know which way was up, much less where they were on the schedule for the show, which had already changed six times in the last two months.

"It's Hardd House!" Robert rubbed his hands together gleefully. "Kiki was shocked when she got the call last month, and they were very specific that this was the only weekend they could shoot. Can you guess why?"

Katherine looked at a giddy Robert and shook her head as her stomach fell. Alistair had said yes. Why had he said yes? She turned around to look back at the house, her mind spinning. This was where Alistair had grown up, and this would be his house one day. Whatever she had pictured in her mind over the years, this was not it.

She felt a little sick.

"It was the only week that Mason and Cassandra Stevens were available, and they wanted to co-host." Robert laughed. "Mason and Cassandra Stevens! I think they are related to the earl somehow."

"The senior earl is Mason Stevens's brother, is senior earl the right term?" Kiki asked.

"No, Bryce Stevens is the current earl. His son, who hasn't officially inherited the title yet, is just referred to as your grace." Claire explained, having done her homework. "I hear that the son, Alistair Stevens, is a dream to look at," she sighed.

Her comment made Katherine's hackles rise for some reason. Claire was new to the crew, and she and Katherine hadn't hit it off, but Katherine hadn't thought much about the girl until now.

Taking her time, Katherine looked Claire over. She was young, pretty, and petite, with a blond pixie cut and big blue eyes.

"This is going to be so much fun! And to think we're the first official film crew allowed to film in the house!" J.D. was just as excited as Robert. Kiki and Claire looked pleased as well, and she could hear them discussing Alistair in soft voices with their heads bent together.

Katherine looked back at the house with conflicted emotions. She was excited to get a peek inside Alistair's home but worried about seeing him again. They had left everything unresolved, and she was concerned about which Alistair she would get. Would he be the serious one, who resented them being there, or the happy Alistair, who went with the flow and didn't let much bother him?

It only took them a moment to finish the short drive to the house, and Katherine was amazed at how massive the house was up close. It looked large from the drive, but standing beside it was overwhelming. She turned to look back at the lush, rolling, green lawn that stretched before the house, wondering if it had looked the same as it did now three hundred years ago when it had been built.

The doors to the house were opened, and a man and a woman dressed in formal clothing came down the stairs to welcome them. It wasn't anyone Katherine knew, so she guessed they were the staff.

"It's just like freaking Downton Abby!" Claire squeaked.

"Welcome to Hardd House," the man said with a little bow, and Claire squeaked again while Katherine felt sick. The two people before her were very different from Abby. "I'm Jackson, and this is my wife, Reva. We run the house for his Grace."

"His Grace!" Kiki said with awe to Claire.

The team had been to several grand houses over the years, but many had been converted into hotels or were open to the public to generate revenue for their upkeep. If they were still owned by the wealthy, titled families of yore, they were never around when they filmed.

Despite this house's grandeur, the way they were greeted made it feel like it was still a family home, which It still was as far as Katherine knew. Jackson led the way into the house after telling them not to worry about their luggage and equipment. It would be unloaded with the utmost care.

J.D., who usually had a fit when anyone touched his stuff, seemed all right with the instructions as he followed the others into the house. They all stopped in their tracks and looked up at the great hall they had just entered. It was a massive space that rose three stories with balconies running around three sides and an enormous center staircase at one end. There was a large fireplace that they could all stand in on one side with limited seating in front of it.

"To your left is his Grace's study, and next to it is the blue drawing room. To your right is the dining room. If the ladies will follow Reva, she'll show you your rooms. If the men will follow me, I'll show you to your rooms."

"Katherine." She heard her name called to her left and looked over to find Bryce watching them all as they took in their surroundings. Did his presence mean that Alistair wasn't going to be there? "May I have a moment of your time to discuss some business?" he asked.

Kiki must have recognized him because she stepped forward with her hand out in greeting. "Your Grace, I'm Kiki Mann, head producer of the show. I know it's sometimes confusing to people, but the stars don't handle the business side of things. I do."

Bryce took her hand in his, his face its usual stony mask. "I'm aware of that fact, Ms. Mann. What I need to talk to Katherine about is personal business." He stood to one side, looking at Katherine as he silently bossed her to join him.

When she entered the study, it was to find many of the Stevens lolling about, looking bored, but they perked up when they saw her.

"Katherine!" Grace exclaimed as she rose to greet her. "You look lovely!" Katherine accepted the kiss on the cheek returning it. "Did Bryce just silently boss you?" she laughed. "He used to do that to me all the time."

Katherine looked over at Mason and Cassandra Stevens, who seemed unusually reserved, and nodded. Davis and Laura, who gave her polite smiles, were also there, as was another couple that Katherine didn't recognize.

"This is Norah and Caleb Stevens. Caleb is Bryce's youngest brother. They're only here for a few days before they're off to their next exciting project." Grace introduced. "Alistair got hung up in New York, but he should be here with a few of his cousins this evening."

Katherine felt herself blush at the mention of Alistair's name.

"Lizzy and Trisha mentioned attending, but we talked them down. Trisha would have been so disappointed if you don't find any ghosts." Grace smiled as she returned to her chair.

Katherine could feel all their eyes on her as if expecting her to do a trick or something, and it was disconcerting.

"Was there business you needed to discuss with me?" Katherine turned to Bryce, perched on the edge of his desk, watching her with assessing eyes.

"No, Grace wanted to say hello."

"Oh," Katherine said awkwardly.

"I also wanted to give the others a minute to get to their rooms. They've all been put on the third floor, but we've put you on the second floor with the family. I didn't want to make it too obvious." Grace graciously said.

"Thank you, but you didn't have to go to so much trouble. I would have been fine on the third floor with the others." Katherine blushed again as she realized she sounded ungrateful.

"It wasn't any trouble," Bryce said. "The staff took care of it."

Grace frowned at her husband with displeasure at his rudeness, but Katherine missed it because she felt like she was being tested somehow and had failed.

When there was a knock on the door, she sighed in relief as the awkward silence was broken.

"I'll take Ms. Rhodes to her room now," Reva said as she entered the room.

"Thank you, Reva," Grace nodded. "Katherine, lunch is in about an hour."

Katherine nodded and followed Reva out of the room and up the grand staircase.

This was going to be the worst shoot ever.

Chapter 19

Lunch had been an enjoyable meal. Robert and Kiki had been all about Mason, asking him about his career and technique. Did he prefer directing or acting? They were enthralled by every word that left his mouth.

Katherine had sat next to Norah, who she discovered was a talented artist, and her husband Caleb, who ran a non-profit that helped third-world countries build their infrastructure. They were by far the most fascinating Stevens, and Katherine wondered what it would be like to spend a lifetime traveling the globe and helping the world one small project at a time.

Grace spent the meal charming J.D. and Claire, asking them all about themselves, which they loved, and Bryce looked a bit distracted as he kept looking at his phone.

"We're to have more than we thought," Laura said as she checked her phone as they prepared to leave the table.

"Really?" Cassie said, sounding excited for the first time since Katherine had arrived. "Who?"

"Alice, Rainer, and Beth." Laura supplied as she flipped her phone over.

Katherine could tell they wanted to ask questions but weren't going to while they had an audience, and Katherine could help with that.

"Grace," Katherine leaned around J.D. to look at her concerned face, "perhaps Reva could give us a brief tour of the house, and we could talk with you and Mr. Stevens later about potential rooms we would like to film in?"

"Yes, that sounds like an excellent idea," Kiki said, standing and taking over. "We only have three days, so we really need to lay our plan out tonight so we can start filming tomorrow. We want to do some exterior shots tonight if it's all right with you. There is going to be a full moon."

"Of course," Bryce nodded as Reva appeared by magic.

"Maybe she's the ghost?" Mason whispered sotto voice to the table.

Riva acted as if she hadn't heard as she smiled at the table and waited for the crew to stand and follow her. Katherine turned to leave, but Grace caught her hand and pulled her back into her seat.

"Katherine will catch up with you all in a bit if that's all right?" Grace asked in her sweetest voice. "Riva, will you close the doors behind you, please?"

Riva nodded as she led the others out of the room, and Claire looked over her shoulder at Katherine with suspicion.

"Watch out for that one," Cassie said when the doors were closed.

Katherine nodded her agreement. "If this is family business, I should probably leave," she insisted, trying to stand again, but Cassie and Grace pulled and pushed her back into her chair.

"In case you haven't figured it out yet, Katherine. You are family." Davis smiled at her as he took some of his wife's leftover bread and shoved it into his mouth.

Katherine looked at them all wide-eyed, but they all continued with the conversation.

"Bryce?" Grace turned to look at her husband.

He smiled his honest-to-goodness smile that once again caught Katherine off guard.

"Mave ran away from home. She told them to join us here, help Alistair on his mission, and leave her the hell alone. They were smothering her, and she couldn't take it anymore."

Katherine watched as all the Stevens' faces broke into grins.

"Do we know where she ran away to?" Mason asked, leaning back into his chair, suddenly relaxed, and Cassie reached over and squeezed his arm in happiness.

"I can guess where," Davis said as he looked at them.

"Sam!" several of them said in unison.

"Do you think so?" Laura asked with a frown.

"Yes, not only because he's in Savannah, but he's her favorite person in the world." Davis stood, ending the conversation. "Are you going to let them film you tonight?" he asked Mason.

"Only if I get to dress up like a ghost. I tried convincing Laura to play the woman in white because she's naturally pale, but she wouldn't bite."

"No pun intended," Bryce said from the head of the table, and Katherine looked at him with shock and awe.

"Bryce has a wicked sense of humor when he has a mind to. It's where Alistair gets it from." Grace winked at Katherine as she stood.

"Is there really a woman in white?" Katherine asked, following them all out of the room.

"No," Laura shook her head. "This place will disappoint your crew."

"Unless Mason has his way!" Davis looked over at Mason, who had a thoughtful look as if determining how he could make the place appear haunted.

"If we keep Rainer off the radar, maybe he can be the bumps in the night?" Mason thought aloud.

The others just ignored him as they all went their separate ways. It wasn't difficult for Katherine to catch up with the others, and she received another worrying look from Claire, but she didn't notice it because she was too busy recalling Davis's words.

Was she really family, and what was Alistair's mission? Did it have something to do with her? Was that why they were there? Had he agreed to do something he didn't want to do to get her to come to him?"

Her heart rate sped up at the thought. It was like the story she had heard as a child where a poor woman sold her greatest asset, her hair, to buy her husband a new watch chain, and her husband had sold his greatest asset, his watch, to buy her a ribbon for her hair. It had always been a story that had touched Katherine.

It was what love should be. Of course, one could look at it from a cynic's standpoint, that love had only made them poorer, but Katherine chose to look at the romance of making a great sacrifice for the one you love.

Was that what Alistair was doing for her?

"Katherine, are you listening?" Kiki asked her with a frown.

"Sorry, I am now," she reassured her and did her best to keep the focus on the rest of the tour and not let her mind wander. The house was so vast that it took the rest of the day. Her favorite part was the roof. One had to climb up a medieval stone tower that had been incorporated into the house to reach it, and the amount of history in the stone amazed her.

When she reached the top, she looked over the vast estate. It went on as far as the eye could see. She took in the quiet calmness and slowly fell in love with it. She was reminded of another story she had read. Jane Austen's 'Pride and Prejudice'.

"Of all this, I might have been mistress," she quoted.

"You still could be," Alistair's gentle voice said from behind her.

Katherine spun around and took her time looking at him. He looked tired.

"I don't deserve it." She shook her head.

"I think you do," he shrugged.

Unable to take it any longer, she ran toward him, and he caught her in his arms, holding her close against him in a fierce hug.

"This was worth the trip across the pond," she could hear a smile in his tired voice.

"You don't have to do this. Alistair. We can cancel the entire thing!" She pulled back and looked up at him. "You're not doing this for me, are you?"

Alistair tucked a piece of her hair behind her ear and trailed in fingers down her face.

"I believed you when you said you didn't care if we filmed here. The reason I agreed to it was to trap you here. To have time to prove to you that you belong here, in this world with me, with my family." He lifted her hand

and placed a kiss on her palm. "Is it working? I take it by the greeting you gave me it is?" He gave a sad smile. "If I had known the house would woo you better than I would, I would have invited you here long ago."

"It's not the house, Alistair." She frowned up at him. She didn't want him to think she was using him again.

"Then what?" he sounded curious.

"You're Uncle Davis said I was family and your mother asked me to stay when they were talking about Mave." She swallowed hard at the memory. "It meant a lot."

"I'm glad. You are family. Why do you think my father is your lawyer? He only works for his family."

"I thought he was helping me because you asked him to," Katherine frowned.

Alistair shook his head in disagreement, but what he would have said next was lost.

"Here you are!" Mason called as he pulled out his phone and sent a text.

"I told Davis to bring beer. We need to celebrate!" Mason patted Alistair on the back as Cassie joined them.

I haven't been up here in years," she said as she walked over to the edge and looked at the ground below and smiled. "Do you remember the first time I came up here, Mason?"

"I do. Caleb was drunk, Rainer was hitting on you-"

"He was not hitting on me. He welcomed me into the family. They knew what was happening before we did." Cassie denied.

"All I remember was you poured beer on my head, then Mom came and broke up the party," he reminded her as he put his arms around her shoulders.

"I miss her," Cassie sighed.

"What's the good news?" Alistair asked with a frown.

"Mave ran away and told Rainer, Alice, and Beth to leave her the hell alone," Davis said as he threw Mason a six-pack which he caught with one hand. "They're on their way here now."

"And Mave said they needed to support you on your mission?" Katherine asked. "What mission might that be?" Mason threw Alistair and then Katherine a beer.

"Bryce still buys the cheap stuff," Mason grimaced as he took a sip. "You should work on that as the future earl, Alistair!" Mason said to change the subject.

It only took a few minutes for Caleb, Laura, Bryce, and Grace to join them.

"Where's Norah," Katherine asked Alistair when it was apparent that she wasn't going to join them.

"Probably resting. She has a bad back, and sitting on long plane rides makes it worse sometimes. Either that or she's lost in one of her drawings somewhere." Alistair pulled her close and kissed her head before they joined the others.

Katherine listened to all the good-natured bantering, which felt surreal.

Did this amazing family really feel she was part of them?

Chapter 20

Katherine was just about to head down to join everyone for a pre-dinner drink when there was a knock on the door. She secretly hoped it would be Alistair, but it was Beth instead.

Beth crossed the room and hugged her. "I feel as if I haven't seen you in ages," she greeted.

"You've had a lot going on lately," Katherine responded, attempting to let Beth know she hadn't taken offense to her lack of communication. "How is Mave, by the way?"

"She seems to be bouncing back, but it's mostly all show." Beth started to tear up. "She was badly hurt, and it will take her a while to fully recover."

"Let's not talk about it," Katherine insisted. "Are Wyatt and the girls here too?"

"No." Beth gave a tender smile at the thought of her husband. "He wanted me to have a little downtime, so he sent me here and stayed behind with the girls. Aunt Lizzy and Aunt Trisha have promised to help him entertain them."

"Entertain them?" Katherine said suspiciously. Katherine hoped Trisha was smart enough to keep Beth's girls away from her father. Not that he would hurt them, but she didn't much care for the idea of him entering her world in another way, through her good friend's children.

"Yes, they are sure to be spoiled. When we were kids, a week with Aunt Lizzy and Aunt Trisha meant afternoon tea, the theater, manicures, and soooo much shopping." Beth smiled at the beautiful memories.

"That sounds nice," Katherine said. "I'm sure Wyatt will appreciate the help."

Another knock on the door sounded, and Katherine called for whomever it was to enter.

"Are you ready to go down?" Kiki asked, stopping short when she saw Beth. "Sorry, I didn't mean to interrupt."

"You didn't. We were just catching up. Kiki Mann, this is my good friend Beth Ramsey. Beth Kiki is one of our producers." Katherine watched the two shake hands and then motioned that they all should head downstairs.

"So, Kiki, do you think you will find any ghosts in the family home?" Beth grinned at the thought. "I've never experienced anything, but I'll be curious to see if you do."

"This is your home?" Kiki asked.

"My Uncle Bryce owns it, but we grew up here."

Katherine couldn't help but think that it would have been a great place to grow up.

"That means you're a Stevens?" Kiki asked with a frown.

"Yes, my father is Rainer Stevens." Beth nodded, sounding proud. It wasn't something she told most people upon first meeting them, but since Beth's parents had traveled with her, Kiki would be meeting them in a few moments.

"The reporter?" Kiki's voice rose a few octaves. "Do you think he would be interested in joining us on our investigation as well?"

"As well," Beth frowned, "who else is joining you?"

"So far, only Mason, but there was a hint of Cassie joining us too." Kiki smiled at the thought of having so many famous people joining the show. It would be a banner episode and get high ratings for sure.

"You can ask if you want, but in my experience, my father and Uncle Mason tend to be more trouble than their worth when you stick them in confined spaces together, not to mention I wouldn't trust either one of them in the dark. I'd keep a close eye on Uncle Mason if I were you. Although, he might behave if Aunt Cassie is there."

Katherine hid a smile as she thought about Mason trying to convince Laura to play a ghost.

They reached the blue drawing room and found it full already. Beth made a beeline right for Alistair when she saw him. Katherine frowned when she noted that Claire was already cozied up next to him. She was so close that if he had sat down, she would have been in his lap.

Katherine frowned, and Alistair gave her a wink when he caught it.

"That's him!" Susie Baker, another investigator who had just arrived, hissed as she joined them. Susie had to come separate because of another commitment she had made.

"How was your trip down?" Katherine asked, trying to distract her and Kiki from Alistair's charming grin and sparkling blue eyes.

Katherine felt like she did the first time she had seen him across the room at Beth's birthday party nine years earlier. Her heart had sped up, and her hands were sweating. The power of love was an amazing thing.

"It was fine." She waved the question away and then returned to the important thing, or rather man, in the room.

"That's the young earl! Alistair Stevens!" Susie's whisper had grown, and she heard a cough behind them as Rainer approached.

"Katherine," he said, leaning in and kissing her cheek. "I don't believe I've had the pleasure of meeting your friends."

"Rainer Stevens, this is Kiki and Susie," Katherine introduced, her eyes wandering over to Alistair again.

Rainer immediately started asking the two women questions, drawing them out and distracting them from Alistair, and they couldn't resist his famous face or Stevens charm as they fell into his trap.

"He'll know their life history in less than an hour," Alice said as she kissed Katherine on the cheek. "It's nice to see." She smiled.

"What's nice to see?" Katherine asked, forcing her gaze away from Alistair and focusing her attention on Alice. She was a petite woman, which was emphasized by her husband, Rainer's great size.

"The way you look at Alistair. We were all worried about him finding love more than the others. He has so much to offer, and we were frightened that someone would try to take advantage of that, but the way you look at him is perfect, and the way he looks at you is perfect too." Alice took her hand and squeezed it. "You still look at him like you did the first time you met."

"I still feel the same," Katherine admitted.

"Then why on earth has it taken the two of you nine years to work it out?" Alice frowned.

"Look at him. He's perfect. Then look at me," she grimaced and shook her head.

Alice nodded. "I get it." She looked over her shoulder at Rainer. "Look at him and look at me. I am convinced every woman he meets wants to steal him from me. It's the same with all the women who married a Stevens man. They naturally draw the women to them like moths to a flame."

"How do you live with the worry." Katherine frowned as she thought about a lifetime of worrying about Alistair leaving her.

"I don't worry for the most part. Every Stevens is incredibly loyal, and they do not stray." Alice looked around and then leaned in as if to tell her a secret. Don't tell Beth because it will gross her out, but if I get too worried, I just take him to bed, and it all seems to work itself out again." She winked and wandered off toward Rainer, who looked fascinated by whatever Susie was blathering about.

Katherine looked at the small woman standing next to the still handsome Rainer as he looked down and gave her a tender smile. Did Alistair really look at her with love?

"Good Lord, the girl can talk about herself," Kiki said grumpily as she rejoined Katherine.

"How do you know so many people in this family?" Kiki curiously asked.

Katherine shrugged as if it was no big deal. "Beth's husband, Wyatt Ramsey, and I grew up together. He introduced me to Beth, who introduced me to

Laura Stevens, my agent. When I first moved to New York, I was also Beth's roommate. I met most of the family through her or Laura."

"Hmmm," Kiki murmured. "The young earl, what do you know about him?" Her eyes were raking over Alistair as if he was snack food.

"What do you want to know?" Katherine asked. She didn't want to share anything about Alistair, but she had to play it cool, and it was a safer bet not to offer any more information than needed. She wanted to tell Claire, Kiki, and Susie to back off. He was hers.

Was he hers?

"Is he in a serious relationship, engaged? What does he do? Where does he go?" Kiki's eyes narrowed as Claire's arm slipped through his as she pulled him closer to say something.

Katherine only shrugged. Next, Kiki would want to know about his bank account.

Laura joined them and handed Katherine a drink.

"Katherine, would you join Bryce and me for a moment? We have something we need to discuss." Laura took Katherine's arm and steered her toward Bryce and Grace, standing alone by the window.

"What are you two talking about with those worried expressions?" Laura asked when they reached their side. "I had to save Katherine, getting the third degree from Kiki about Alistair, and you were my excuse."

"Grace is worried about what Mason has planned for this weekend." Bryce gave an amused smile as he sipped his drink.

"And you're not?" Grace asked with a frown.

"No, he'll charm his way out of whatever mishaps occur. He always does."
Bryce even sounded amused, which changed from his usual serious expression, and Grace must have thought so as well because she tilted her head
and looked at him as a slow smile emerged.

"You're actually looking forward to this, aren't you?" she asked, but before
he could answer, dinner was announced. "Saved by the bell," Grace muttered as she shook her head.

Chapter 21

Dinner was a success. Many different conversations were going on, and Katherine, sitting between Beth and Caleb, didn't lack for things to talk about. She spent the first half of dinner catching up with Beth and the second half talking with Caleb about his latest project. In between it all, she kept sneaking glances at Alistair, sitting between Kiki and Susie. The closest poor Claire could get to him was across the table, but it seemed fair since she had monopolized him before dinner.

After dinner, they all moved back to the drawing room, where the conversation continued over coffee. Katherine had been cornered by Robert, who wanted to take a few moments to review the shots he wanted that evening. She nodded to him as she listened to his ideas while her eyes strayed to Alistair again.

"Not you too!" Robert said as he rolled his eyes. "What is it about the young future earl that draws every woman he meets to him?"

"I couldn't say what draws every woman to him, and I'm sure there are a few who aren't drawn to him," Katherine said, not realizing that she sounded unconvinced by her statement.

"You can't even say that convincingly," Robert said as he turned to study Alistair head-on, not caring that he was openly staring.

"He is handsome and has charisma," Robert thought aloud before he took a sip of his coffee.

"And he is a future earl, rich, and really good at making money," Rainer said from behind him, studying Alistair while he sipped his coffee too.

"True," Robert said, nodding.

"He's also funny on occasion," Davis joined in the conversation, and the others around them started to take notice and turned to look at Alistair as well.

Half of the room had turned in his direction and was assessing him as he spoke to his mother. Claire, Susie, and Kiki had found others to talk with for a change, leaving Alistair free to speak with his mother about something that looked important.

"You should marry him, Katherine," Cassie said with a grin, "before one of the other ladies snag him first."

Alistair looked up at that moment, caught half the room watching him, and frowned at their sudden attention.

"Is there a problem?" he loudly asked across the vast room, catching everyone's attention.

"No, sweetie, we were just trying to determine what makes you so irresistible to some women." Cassie lifted her cup of coffee toward him as his frown deepened at the thought of being irresistible.

"All women," Robert snorted, disagreeing with Cassie's statement that it was only some women.

"Not all women." Alistair shook his head as his eyes met Katherine's across the room, the message clear that she didn't find him irresistible.

Robert snorted. "If you mean Katherine by that statement, you're one hundred percent wrong. She's been staring at you all night."

Katherine stomped on his foot, and he shouted in pain. "Stop it! You may not be as overt about it as the other three, but you have been staring at him." Robert had given up all semblance of tact, and it caused Claire, Susie, and Kiki to gasp in protest.

Katherine took a deep breath and set her coffee cup on one of the trays. "Are you ready to shoot, Robert?" she asked, changing the subject as the other three women's eyes narrowed and looked like they would do bodily harm to either her or Robert. After all, one of them was in charge of her make-up and could easily make her look like a clown if she wanted.

"In about an hour," he said, looking at his watch, clueless about the danger he was in.

"Then I'll go get changed," Katherine said to no one in particular as she turned to leave and immediately faced a wall of Stevenses, who all looked at her with knowing grins that said she could run, but she couldn't hide because it was a family affair now. "Excuse me," she whispered as she pushed past them.

Katherine was halfway up the massive staircase when Alistair caught her elbow and pulled her behind him. Many of the Stevens family had blocked the door keeping her co-workers in the drawing room.

"Don't fight it, dear. It's what the Stevens men do. We pull our women behind us until we have them where we want them, which is never a bad place to be unless you're Cassie!" Caleb called.

"Alistair!" she hissed as he pulled her down the long gallery and toward the door that was her room for her stay. He opened it and pushed her through, closing it swiftly behind him. How did you know which room I was staying in?" she asked, out of breath at the suddenness of his actions.

"It's my house. I chose the room I wanted you in, which is right next to mine." He walked toward her, pushing her back with his intensity before his hands reached out and grabbed her arms to hold her in place. "I have been watching you watch me all night, and all I have wanted to do was kiss you." He looked at her lips as she licked them in anticipation.

"You realize you gave us away, and now all my co-workers know that you and I have a thing, right?" she asked.

"A thing?" he repeated, "Hmmm, I was hoping by longing looks were more meaningful than a thing." He pulled her body flush with his.

"I don't think the others wanted to acknowledge your longing looks if there really were any," Katherine let her body lean into his. She had missed him so much, and they still had a lot to talk about, but having him so close was heaven.

"If there were any?" he repeated what Katherine said again, giving her a little shake. "It is all I have been doing all night!"

"I never saw a single longing look," Katherine shrugged, enjoying flirting with him again. It used to be something they were adept at before the last year when life got in the way.

He let his eyes trace the curves of her face as he cradled her head in his hands, and his intense look made her weak-kneed. When he brought his thumb up to her lips and traced them, she couldn't help the sigh that escaped her lips.

"How's this for longing looks," he smiled tenderly.

"Oh, Alistair," she shook her head as tears threatened. "I missed you so much, and I'm still very much afraid that you will wake up and choose someone else."

"Sweetheart, you are my heart," he whispered before his lips caught hers in a gentle kiss.

There was a sudden knock on her door, and Alistair cursed as he stepped back.

"Who is it?" Katherine called in an unsteady voice. Her eyes were glued to Alistair's. She was unwilling to look away first.

"It's Claire, Katherine. I need to do your make-up for the shoot," Claire called through the thick door.

"I have to change first. Can you come back in ten minutes?" She cleared her throat to make her voice louder. Then she turned to Alistair with a glare. "Obviously, your looks weren't longing enough because Claire didn't get the point."

Alistair's response was to kiss her again before she wrenched herself away.

"I have to change now!" she stepped back from him as jealousy ate at her core. He was here with her now, which should be enough, but there were so many unspoken words between them that she was still in doubt.

"Go ahead," he said as he crossed the room and sat in a chair.

"No!" A year ago, she would have been thrilled at the idea of him watching her change, but now she wanted some space until she could figure out how to ask all the questions she wanted to ask. The primary one being what had changed between him and his family. "Claire will want to do my makeup in here, and you can't be here for that!"

"Why not? I can sit here and look at you longingly while she does." Alistair let Katherine pull him from the chair and push him toward the door. "Fine, I'll leave, but you'll give me one more kiss."

Katherine stopped with her hand on the doorknob and looked up at him. This time, her look was filled with longing before his lips claimed hers.

When he ended the kiss, he rested his head against hers. "We're almost there. I can feel it," he took her hand and rested it against his chest as Katherine nodded her agreement.

"Now go!" she insisted as she wrenched open the door and pushed him out before she changed her mind.

They were almost there. They were only one good conversation away.

Chapter 22

A listair felt they were only a conversation away from solving all their worries, but his family was the problem that was blocking that conversation. He had brought his family in to help woo her, but now they were in the way, and alone time with Katherine this weekend might be next to impossible.

He supposed he could sneak into her room after everyone went to sleep, but he didn't want anything they did to be in secret anymore. Which meant an open conversation in a usual way, and the next time he made love to her, he would have all of her for keeps. He was determined on that point.

Alistair wandered back down the stairs and into his father's study, where he flopped into a chair across from his mother, who was curled up watching a program on her tablet.

"What are you watching?" Alistair asked as he heard a scream.

"Some of Katherine's show. I wanted to know what to expect." Grace's eyes were glued to the screen. "I give credit to Katherine. She's calm through all the other's antics." They watched for a while before Grace placed her tablet on the table next to her and turned her attention to her son. "Did you two figure it all out yet?"

The door opened, and Bryce entered carrying a tray of coffee with two cups for him and his wife.

"No, but we're a little closer, and your plan of making her feel included feels as if it's breaking the ice a little." Alistair stood, realizing that his parents were hoping for a little alone time. "I'll go keep an eye on everyone," he suggested.

There was a knock on the door, and Bryce called for whomever it was to enter with a resigned sigh.

Reva entered with Mason and Cassie's daughter Poppy hot on her heels, and behind her was a huge man who towered over his small cousin while looking just as resigned as his father.

"Poppy!" Grace greeted her as she stood to give her a warm hug and a kiss on the cheek. "Reva, will you go and find Mason and Cassie? I think they would like to know that their daughter has come to visit."

Poppy's eyes grew large as she looked at Grace. "Mom and Dad are here?"

"Isn't that why you came?" Bryce asked as he eyed the man behind Poppy, who, to his credit, eyed him right back.

"No, I wanted to talk with Uncle Bryce and Alistair about a few things. It's business."

An awkward silence descended as they all looked at each other.

"Poppy, will you introduce me to your friend?" Alistair said, holding out his hand in greeting.

The man took his hand, and his handshake was firm.

"Umm," Poppy tucked a stray piece of strawberry red hair behind her ear and licked her lips, her brown eyes darting nervously to the man behind her.

"Isaac Harrison, this is my Aunt Grace and Uncle Bryce Stevens, and this is their son Alistair." She took a breath. "Isaac is my husband."

There was a stunned silence, and Grace was the one to break it first. "Congratulations!" she said, hugging Poppy again and then Isaac in his turn. Isaac accepted the hug and then shook Bryce's extended hand.

"I wish I could say a surprise spouse was a new event for this family, but it's not." Grace smiled, attempting to put everyone at ease.

"It's not?" Poppy asked.

"No, your Uncle Caleb and Aunt Norah were married for three years before he broke the news to us, and that was only because your Aunt Lizzy forced his hand." As Grace finished her statement, Cassie and Mason swept into the rooms all smiles.

Alistair took that moment to slip out and close the door behind him. He knew there was a good story, and he was eager to hear it, but he didn't want to be part of the drama about to unfold. Aunt Cassie would probably take it in stride, but Uncle Mason would not.

Alistair turned as Katherine descended the staircase. She wore a cuddly sweater highlighting her curves, a long skirt, and boots. Her hair was pulled into a tight ponytail, and her makeup highlighted her unique bone structure.

"You look perfect as if you were made to descend that staircase as the lady of the house," Alistair whispered in her ear as she joined him, and he enjoyed the blush that even her makeup couldn't hide.

"I doubt that." Katherine shook her head and allowed him to tuck her hand in the crook of his arm.

"Where are we headed?" he asked.

"Outside, we're doing the exterior shots." She nodded in the direction of the front door, and Alistair led her to it, then opened the door to a set of blazing lights with her crew gathered around.

"That was perfect. Can you do it one more time!" Kiki asked.

"Why?" Alistair asked with a frown.

"Because we want to get some shots of the two of you walking around the site as you tell her a few stories, and we want it to appear as if it took all day," Kiki explained without really paying attention to what she was saying.

"No, work with the shot you got if it was perfect," he smiled a tight smile that didn't reach his eyes, and he could tell it made Katherine nervous, so he tried to relax. It was going to be a total circus, as he had feared.

"Where's Mason? We will need him soon." Kiki moved on to the next item.

"You'll have to film without him. Some unexpected family business cropped up." Alistair squeezed Katherine's hand and then stepped away from her. "I'll watch from the shadows."

He didn't want to miss his chance to see Katherine in action, so he moved into the darkness behind the crew and watched as she transformed before his eyes.

All at once, she became all business, walking and talking to the camera as she said the most ridiculous things, but they sounded almost sane when she said them. It went on for hours, with her walking and talking as they caught different angles of the house behind her.

When they called it for the night, it was past two in the morning, and the house was quiet.

"Is everything all right with Mason?" Katherine asked with a worried frown.

"Why? Are you afraid he won't be able to do the show?" It was out as soon as he thought it, and he wasn't sure why he had said it, but he wanted to take it back immediately.

Katherine stopped breathing for a moment, and he watched as she looked at something in the distance over his shoulder while swallowing hard as she reined in her emotions.

"Of course, that's what it is," she agreed and turned to leave.

Dammit! Why had he said it?

"Katherine!" he reached out and grabbed her arm to keep her from walking away.

"We're both tired, Alistair. We'll talk some more tomorrow if I have the time." She nodded in his direction without meeting his eyes and then walked away and into the house.

"Where had that anger come from, and why had it come on so quickly?" he rubbed his face in frustration. He had been so worried about Katherine figuring it all out that he hadn't stopped to check himself and make sure he didn't have to figure anything out, and it was apparent he did.

When he entered the house, he noticed the door to the study was open, and the light was still on, so he wandered in to find his father sitting behind his desk.

"I take it by the look on your face that it didn't go as well as you thought it would?" he asked as he looked up from what he was reading.

"No, I suddenly became very angry with her when I wasn't." Alistair shook his head in confusion.

Bryce smiled but didn't say anything.

"What, I take it you have a guess?" Alistair asked in a bitter voice that his father ignored.

"You need her to need you, and she hasn't confirmed that she does. I would guess that watching her tonight has only strengthened your doubt that she does need you." He looked back at his papers as Alistair mulled over his words.

Was that really what it was all about? He needed Katherine to want and need him? He rubbed his face once more. He needed something else to think about. Some separation from the subject may give him a little clarity.

"What happened with Poppy's bombshell?" Alistair asked.

"Cassie was briefly hurt but managed to push past it." Bryce made a note on the paper in front of him.

"And Uncle Mason?" Alistair asked, feeling sorry for Poppy and at the same time jealous that she had found her love and married him. No doubt that had something to do with his sudden anger too. Nine years was a long time to wait.

"Unusually quiet." Bryce frowned as he said it. It was evident that he was worried about his brother's reaction. "Poppy wants us to consult on a few things. There are children involved."

"There never were any half-measures with Poppy, were there?" Alistair rose.

"She's too much like her mother and father in that regard."

"We'll talk about it tomorrow, and you'll tell me how I can help?"

"Yes," Bryce said, not looking up as his son left him hard at work.

Alistair knew his father was as worried as Uncle Mason was and wouldn't be able to sleep even if he tried.

Alistair felt that sleep would be a stranger to him as well, and maybe some quiet time to think would help him sort a few things out before seeing Katherine in the morning.

Chapter 23

Katherine had been shooting most of the day, and she was exhausted. Not surprisingly, she hadn't slept well as she tossed and turned, wondering what had suddenly changed with Alistair. She had so much hope since she arrived, but it all disappeared instantly when she asked about his uncle.

The weather had gotten much colder overnight, and she was wearing the same thing she had the previous evening for continuity, which meant that she had spent most of the day shivering between takes. She needed a walk to clear her head and warm up, so when they stopped filming to grab some lunch, Katherine wandered off toward a stand of trees in the distance that looked peaceful.

She was halfway across the clearing when Alistair caught up with her, grabbing her arm to stop her.

"Let me go. Alistair." It was softly spoken, and she meant that he should let go of more than just her arm. He should let her go. It was evident that it would never work between them. A brief meet-up every year or so with no complications or commitment seemed the best they could hope for moving forward.

"No, Katherine. I will never let you go. I can't." He understood her point but disagreed with her.

"Fine, then let's go back to what we used to be. A few meetings a year, where we enjoy each other's company and then go about our lives." Katherine looked up at him with pleading eyes. "This isn't going to work any other way, and last night proves it. Whenever we finally fall on the same page and let our guard down, one of us freaks out and hurts the other, and I can't keep going through that."

She wrenched her arm away from his and took off, walking briskly until she reached the trees.

"Katherine, stop!" he called, and she did for a moment to turn toward him.

"I love you, Alistair. I love you, not your money or title or family. You're the only one for me, but it won't work for us in a traditional sense, so we have to figure out what will work and what we had will because it worked for over nine years."

"No, Katherine, that won't work for me. I want you there when I have a bad day. I want you there when, like last night, my cousin drops the bomb that she's married without telling everyone. I want you to travel with me and have children with me. I need a partner. I want us to always be together in every sense of the word, and I believe it can work in a traditional sense and agree that we only have to figure out what we need to do to make it work."

"It's too hard. We shouldn't have to work on having a relationship! It should come naturally, and ours doesn't." She shook her head and started walking again.

He grabbed her and pulled her close. "Katherine, from the moment I looked at you, I wanted you, and it was the same for you. That has never waned, which is the most natural thing in the world. All the other stuff is my ego and your emotional baggage getting in the way. Neither one of us is perfect, but up until this last year, we've only had perfect moments together. That confuses things. All relationships take work, and we must ask ourselves if we are worth the work, and I know we are."

Katherine looked at Alistair and thought about having him in her life forever, then she reached out and touched his cheek right before there was a sudden creaking, and the ground below her gave way. She tried to reach for Alistair, but suddenly he wasn't there, and she was surrounded by darkness as her world spun. After a moment, the air whooshed back into her lungs with a sharp pain that made her cry out. She closed her eyes and steadied her breath while she tried to reach for her phone in her skirt pocket. When she felt it, she shook it, and the flashlight turned on, which made her feel marginally better.

She heard a groan next to her and jerked her head to look, which caused her to wince in pain. What caused her more pain was seeing Alistair lying next to her with blood oozing from his head.

"Alistair!" she called and slowly moved her arm, which also caused her great pain, to try and shake him awake, but all she got was a groan. 'Please let him be all right,' she thought as her shaky fingers attempted to dial the phone.

The only person she could think to call was Beth.

"Hey, girl, what's up?" Beth said with a smile on her face. "I've been watching the shoot covertly from the shadows, and it appears to be going well. You look amazing."

"Beth," she croaked.

"Katherine! What's wrong? Where are you!" Beth's happy voice suddenly turned urgent as she heard the pain and distress in Katherine's.

"It's Alistair; he's been hurt," Katherine couldn't hold back the tears as she turned her head to look at his unconscious form.

"You too, by the sound of it. Where are you?" Katherine could hear her walking and opening doors. "I'm putting you on speaker. Tell us what's going on."

"I don't know where we are, it's dark, and I can't see anything." Katherine shook her head and winced again. "We were walking and taking, and then the ground gave way, and we both fell." Katherine felt tears rolling down her cheeks. "Alistair is unconscious, and I can't get him to wake up."

"Where were you walking, Katherine?" Bryce's voice asked. Beth had joined some of the other Stevens, but Katherine couldn't see was the SOS text going out to the family and how they were quickly filling up the study to find out what was happening.

"I saw a stand of trees and wanted to get away," Katherine said, suddenly feeling tired.

"Which direction, Katherine!" Bryce demanded.

"I don't remember, but it only took me a few minutes to walk to where we are. I'm very tired." She said, her eyes starting to droop.

"Stay awake, Katherine!" Rainer said. "Don't fall asleep. We'll be there soon."

"Mmmm," she muttered before she fell unconscious.

Beth ended the call and tried calling her back, but she didn't answer. Then she tried Alistair's phone with little result.

"What are we going to do?" Beth asked as she looked around at all the worried Stevens' faces.

"We're going to find them," Rainer said as he looked at Bryce.

"I can help," Isaac said, stepping forward. "I have some experience in search and rescue."

"Thank you, Isaac. That would be greatly appreciated." Bryce nodded as he gave Grace a quick hug while Rainer grabbed a map of the grounds and laid it out on the table.

"Do you know of any old wells or subterranean caverns?" Isaac asked as he approached the map. "Does anyone know the last place she was seen?"

The conversation continued for a few moments, with everyone getting more and more concerned by the minute. It wasn't going to be as easy as they thought, not unless their fall had left a great gaping hole in the ground, which wouldn't be the case if it was dark where they were.

"We'll start here and fan out." Isaac pointed to a place on the map closest to where Katherine had last been seen. "Beth, you keep calling their phones to see if you can get them to answer and let us know if you have any success. Poppy, can you call the local officials and get additional help here? The more people we have looking, the faster we'll find them and get medical help too. They'll need attention as soon as possible if they're both uncon-scious."

"I'll tell Katherine's crew," Grace said as she squeezed Bryce's hand before she left the room.

Poppy looked at her husband, her face pale. "Please find them," she begged, fighting tears, and his only response was to nod, his expression devoid of emotion. If the others thought the interaction was odd, no one said anything.

Everyone was happy to have Isaac take over and were eager to start search-ing because it was better than waiting around.

Chapter 24

W hen Katherine opened her eyes again, it was to find Alistair leaning over her and calling her name.

"Thank God!" he swore when she opened her eyes and looked up at him.

"You're alive," she whispered as she tried to reach up and stroke his face, but as soon as she lifted her arm, she cried out in pain.

"Where does it hurt?" he asked as his eyes skimmed her battered body.

"Everywhere," she whispered because even talking hurt. "I thought you were dead." Katherine felt tears start to fall at the thought of never seeing Alistair again. "I don't think I could manage with this life if you weren't in it."

"And it only took falling two stories through rotted floorboards to figure that out," Alistair teased as he squeezed her hand.

"I knew a long time ago," she denied. "Are you all right?" Katherine looked up and down his body, searching for injury.

"I took a significant hit to my head and have a doozy of a headache, but otherwise, only a few bruises. You, unfortunately, hit a set of stairs when you fell, which made your landing rougher than mine." Alistair looked at her once more, trying to assess the damage. "Can you wiggle your fingers and toes?"

Katherine attempted to do both and was successful. "Yes."

Alistair then gently ran his hands over her body and noted where she would cry out or wince. "I think you have some broken ribs, a dislocated shoulder, a broken leg, and you hit your head pretty hard too, but that's all I can see on the outside." He frowned at the thought of what could be on the inside.

"If I'm broken beyond repair, will you still love me?" Katherine meant it as a joke, but her voice broke at the end.

"I love you, Katherine, but you'll be fine." He squeezed her hand again.

"I called Beth, and they're looking for us," Katherine said as the memory of her conversation with Beth flooded back.

"I know, they've found us, and now they're figuring out how to get to us. Some rather large trees fell across the dirt that followed us through the hole." As if sensing that he was talking about them, his phone rang, and he answered it.

"Katherine's awake, and you're on speaker," he told whomever it was on the other end.

"Oh, thank God! Are you all right, Katherine?" Grace's voice asked.

"She's holding her own but can't talk well because she has broken ribs." Alistair gave her a reassuring smile. "Does it look like we'll be out of here anytime soon?"

"I'm not sure. They are going slow because it's all like a giant house of cards. They're worried that if they move the wrong thing, it will make matters worse." Grace paused as she said the words. She must be scared to death for her son.

"Thank goodness Poppy's husband has search and rescue experience. It's as if he was sent to us from above to help." Grace cleared her throat.

"Maybe he was," Alistair agreed. "You'll have to give me the details when we're out of this hole. You don't happen to know what this hole is, do you?" It was dark, and neither Katherine nor Alistair could make out anything more than a foot in front of them.

"Beth and Poppy started digging through the old maps at the house and found one that listed a manor house in the spot about five hundred years ago. It probably had a partial basement kitchen. The entire site sits on a small hill, which is probably the house ruins covered in dirt and vegetation. I'm surprised I didn't find it when I was digging on the property years ago." Someone shouted in the background. "I have to go, Alistair. I don't want to run the battery on your phone down."

"Good idea, Mom. I turned Katherine's off for now, and we'll turn it back on if mine dies. I love you."

"I love you too, and you, Katherine, we all love and are worried about you too. Both of you, please be careful and don't take any chances." Then she ended the call, probably so they wouldn't hear her cry.

"Tell me about your mom and dad?" Katherine asked, closing her eyes against her throbbing head.

"I don't know all of it, but I do know that they met at a fundraising party for the university where my mom was teaching. She crashed the party to ask some old earl if she could do an archeological dig on his land. She was shocked to discover that the old earl wasn't so old and was very handsome."

Katherine sighed at the romantic image of the story placed in her head.

"They were carefully neutral with each other at first, and then they suddenly fell in love, but my dad fought it. He said it was because he didn't want or have time for a full-time relationship, but I am guessing that he was worried my mom wouldn't want all the headaches that came with being the head of the family and an earl."

"Do you worry about that with me?" It sounded so familiar, and, in a way, it was what Katherine worried about also. She feared she wouldn't be able to handle all the responsibilities she would have because of his position.

"No, it's a job and a job that is similar to the one you already do. I know you can handle it, so I didn't hesitate to ask you to marry me. To be clear, it wasn't that my dad thought mom couldn't perform the job. He worried she would eventually resent the time it took to perform it."

"How did she learn to cope?" Katherine desperately needed to hear the answer.

"She had her own life. She did her thing, and Dad did his. They did some things together, but for the most part, they supported each other equally in all things." Alistair squeezed her hand. "It's how it could be with us. I don't want you to give anything up. I only want our lives to be lived together."

Katherine felt more tears fall. She wanted that too.

"I don't want us ever to hate each other. My biggest fear is that all these perfect moments that you talk about have given you a false sense of who I am and that when you get to know the real, insecure, and neurotic me, you won't want me anymore, and that would kill me." Katherine's voice was barely a whisper as she said aloud what she feared most.

"But it wouldn't kill you to give up before we even try?" he asked in a patient voice.

"If I walked away before you hated me, there would always be a little hope; if I knew you hated me, there would be no hope." She squeezed her eyes closed, attempting to stop the tears.

"Is this that neurotic part you don't want me to see?"

Katherine smiled.

"You realize none of that makes sense, right?"

"It makes sense to me because it's what happened to my parents." Katherine swallowed hard at the memories. "He was so cruel to her and looking back. I can now see it for what it was, hate."

"Oh sweet, he didn't hate her because of who she was; he hated her because she had all the power and money in the relationship, and she wasn't easily controlled like he thought she would be. That would never happen to us." He shook his head.

"How do you know? How can you be sure?" Katherine opened her eyes and searched for him in the darkness, but she couldn't see him.

He was about to say something when the earth around them started to shake, and stones began to fall.

Alistair did his best to cover her body to shield her from the worst without causing her broken body any more injury, but he lost his balance and fell across her legs, which shot pain through her body and caused her to black out once more.

Chapter 25

When Katherine next awoke, it was to hear Alistair's deep baritone singing the Christmas carol, 'I'll Be Home for Christmas' his voice was lovely, and Katherine listened to him for a few moments until be realized she was awake.

"Good, you're awake again. How are you doing?" he asked as he took her hand and squeezed it.

"I'm all right," she lied because what was she going to say? Everything hurt, and she wanted to die. "You have a nice voice, but why a Christmas carol?"

"Thank you, and because I love Christmas, it makes me happy."

"I didn't know that." Katherine thought about all the time they had spent together, which had never been during the holidays. She felt that it was one more thing she didn't know about him that she probably should.

"I want to ask you a question about something you said earlier?" Alistair said, and Katherine gave a shiver because it was getting colder.

"All right," she agreed.

"You said you already know you couldn't live without me, and if that's the case, why do you keep pushing me away? Why are you pushing me away if I mean so much to you?" Alistair stroked her cheek.

"I told you earlier that it's because of hope. If I walk away, there's always a chance you'll be there, but if you walk away, you won't come back." Her voice cracked at the thought of it. "I might ask you the same thing. Why do you push me away if I mean so much to you." When he didn't respond, she needed to give an example. "What happened last night when I asked about Mason, you pushed me back with your nasty comment, and when you accused me of making up the fact that I was so innocent, that was pushing me away again. Why?"

"My Dad pointed it out to me last night. I always push you away when you show strength. I need you to need me, and I fear that if you ever decide that you don't need me, you won't want me."

"How was I showing strength last night?" Katherine frowned as she tried to understand what had happened.

"It's tied into your fear. You saw your parents grow to hate each other because of money, but, my love, I will always make sure you have your own wealth and never need mine. It's what I do, and I can reason that you will always need me to do that, but last night I saw you in your element. I realized that even if I can't make you money, you can and will support yourself through your career, and it made me realize that you don't need me as much as I believed you did."

Katherine thought about what he said, and while it made her happy that he saw her strengths, it made her angry that he didn't believe that she needed him for love.

"Alistair, I need you like I need air. It has nothing to do with money. I need to know that there will always be another tomorrow and that you will always be there, even when I'm at my worst. It has nothing to do with money. It never did. Unlike my mother, you have all the power in this relationship." Her voice broke in its sincerity.

Alistair stroked her hair back from her face. "Katherine, believe me when I say, in every way, you have and will always have all the power in this relationship. All you ever have to do is ask for the smallest thing, and I will make sure it's yours." Alistair stroked her cheek and wiped a tear. "Perhaps we're looking at this all wrong. Maybe it's not about needing so much as trusting and relying on each other for strength and support."

"Maybe we both need each other equally," Katherine suggested.

"There's no maybe about it," Alistair shook his head before kissing her lips gently.

"Alistair, I have one more question," Katherine asked after he sat back and stroked her hair again.

"Yes, my love," he asked.

"At lunch yesterday, Davis said your family was here to help you with a mission. What is the mission?" Katherine tried to look meek as she secretly hoped it was her.

"It's your family too, and your the mission, my love," she could hear the smile in his voice. "Mom helped me plan it. She told me that my grandmother was one of the most important people in bringing her and my dad together. Because of her, Mom felt accepted and wanted. Her support meant that she was part of the family. She felt that maybe she could pay it forward and let you know how important you have become to our family over the years."

"I have?" Katherine asked.

"You have. Even without me, you will always be a part of the family. Once you're in, it's not so easy to escape it." He laughed, and it was as if the heavens opened. There was a creaking sound, and then a sliver of light as the debris over them was lifted.

Katherine felt her heart opening up in much the same way. Was it as simple as Alistair's family wanting her too? She had to admit that being accepted by all the Stevens was a powerful thing to the woman who had been a child that always felt unwanted. Had Grace always felt unwanted when she was a child? Is this what had happened to her also?

"I lied, Alistair," she felt him tense next to her.

"About what, Katherine? We'll work through it no matter what," he insisted, and Katherine smiled at his determined frown. Seeing him in the growing light above was such a beautiful thing.

"Thank you for saying that. It makes me sure." Katherine reached up, wincing but following through as she placed her hand on his neck. Love hurt in so many different ways, but it also soothed the hurt it caused.

"Alistair," she whispered when his face was only an inch from hers, "will you marry me, please." She knew she had to be the one to ask. It was the only way he would ever be sure of her because of how much she had denied him in the past.

A smile lit his face, and he shouted with joy.

"What's going on? Did you get hurt more?" Grace's voice called from above.

"No!" Alistair called back. "Katherine just asked me to marry her! Should I say yes?"

"You'd better!" Cassie hollered back. "I already have a song picked out. Should I sing it now?"

"Yes! I've been waiting nine years to hear our song!" Alistair looked at Katherine's confused look.

"Aunt Cassie picks all our songs. Well, everyone's but Beth and Fiona, they had to do it their own way, but I'm pretty sure she picked it out anyway and never told them about it-"

"Alistair," Katherine cut him off, "you still haven't answered my question."

"Yes! Yes! Yes! I will marry you as soon as we get out of this hole. Dad, can you arrange that!" He hollered up, he couldn't see anyone, but he knew they were all there listening.

"He's already on the phone!" Mason shouted back. "Sing Cassie. We're all dying to know what song you chose."

"Maybe not those words, Dad," Poppy said, and Alistair could hear the eye-roll.

"Sorry, my bad. Waiting to hear what the song choice is, is killing us! Better?" There was silence above for a moment until they heard Mason say, "girl if you roll those eyes any further back, they're gonna stick! That goes for you too, Beth!"

"They're all yours now!" Alistair promised Katherine as Cassie began to sing an old Cole Porter standard, 'Night and Day'.

"We'll dance to it soon, I promise." Then his lips claimed hers, and Katherine sighed, letting go of any more doubts she had. Sometimes you just had to let go and fall into your happiness.

Chapter 26 (The End)

It had been almost two months since the accident. The Stevens family had rallied around Katherine and Alistair, ensuring they had all they needed to recover. The ghost hunt had gone on despite the accident because the family wanted it finished.

Mason had taken over Katherine's hosting duties for the show and turned the entire thing into a farce by saying, 'Did you hear that?', 'Who touched me?' and 'Is this a cold spot?' for every other take. There was even one point where he accused the non-existent ghost of passing gas which then turned into a maybe the ghost did it, perhaps the ghost didn't.

Katherine knew it would be a hit when it finally hit the small screen. No one would care about the house and whether it was haunted. All they would do was see it as a light-hearted episode led by Mason Stevens. There was already talk of inviting him back for the next season if he was interested.

Katherine was almost back to her usual self, she was still careful about doing too much, but she was pleased to be alive and in one piece. Alistair had indeed only received a bump to the head, so his recovery had been much quicker than Katherine's.

One thing she had learned was that he did love Christmas. It was indeed his favorite time of year. Every year the Stevens family picked a different destination for Christmas, and this year, because of Katherine's injuries, they had made the destination London. Not only had the family included Katherine, but they had included her sisters as well.

After the holiday, her sisters returned to New York and stayed at the apartment there. Katherine knew that when she and Alistair returned to New York, they would find a place where they could live. They were still only engaged. They had wanted to be married, but Katherine's injuries were worse than they had thought, and she didn't want to get married from a hospital bed.

Katherine's London apartment was modest but pleasant, and now she bustled around its comfy warmth as she put the final preparations on the meal she still owed Alistair. He had won it fair and square, and it was well past the time that she should have delivered.

It was a simple meal of steak, French fries, salad, and milkshakes. She had taken time with her appearance and was wearing a simple blue dress with her hair pulled back in a high ponytail. Her leg and foot still weren't one hundred percent healed, and she was in a boot, so fancy shoes were out for the time being.

She was lighting the last candle when there was a knock on the door, and she took one last look around before she moved to open it. Only when she opened it, it wasn't Alistair. It was George.

He didn't greet her as he pushed past her into the apartment, looking for something or someone. "Where are they?"

"Who?' Katherine asked, knowing very well he wanted to know where her sisters were.

"Your sisters!"

"They aren't here." Katherine shook her head, watching as he walked through all the rooms, turning on all the lights as he went. "Don't forget to look under the bed!" she called. She was no longer afraid of him or cared what he thought. The Stevens family had taught her about a real family, and he had never been her real family, so what he thought didn't matter.

"But you know where they are, don't you!" He charged her and got right up in her face, but Katherine stood her ground.

"If I do, I'm not about to tell you." She shrugged. "But while you're here, I do have a question. You don't happen to know who my real father is, do you?" It was worth a shot, not that she expected him to answer.

George looked around him, taking in her appearance and the candles on the table. "Are you expecting company?"

"Yes, my fiancé is coming for dinner."

"Funny, I don't see a ring." George looked pointedly at her finger.

"No, not yet," Katherine agreed.

"He probably doesn't really want you. Who would? He only wants the money." George smiled maliciously at her.

"That's something you know all about, isn't it?" Katherine fired back, suddenly weary of him.

"Is everything all right, Katherine?" Alistair asked. He had entered through the door she had left open when George had arrived.

"Everything's fine, Alistair. George was just leaving." She looked at Alistair with a smile, pleased to see him. He looked very handsome in his suit and tie. He must have come straight from the office. "You look nice."

"Thank you, my love. You look nice as well." He smiled back, and they were content to look at each other for a moment.

"This is your fiancé," George snorted.

"Yes," Katherine's smile grew.

"He's too cheap even to get you a ring. Either that or he'll use your money to buy it for you." George started toward the door, but Alistair stopped him.

"One thing before you go, Randolph. Katherine and her sisters no longer wish to see you. They are under the protection of my extensive and protective family, which includes Trisha Livingston. I would advise you to let it be. You can leave your information with my father, Bryce Stevens, and if they wish to contact you, they will do so through him."

"You can't do that! They are my daughters!" George spat.

"They're adults, and it's their wish to have nothing to do with you for the time being."

A tense silence descended on the room as he eyed them. He must have decided they were serious because he abruptly turned and walked out, slamming the door behind him.

"That was unpleasant," Alistair said as he took off his coat and threw it on a chair, then walked toward her and took her in his arms. "Are you all right?"

"I'm fine," Katherine assured him as she kissed him. "I've discovered that he doesn't matter all that much anymore. I did ask him if he knew who my real father was, though, but he didn't answer." Katherine frowned, realizing he hadn't answered.

"We'll hire someone to figure it out. How does that sound?" he asked as he looked around.

"I would like that," she said, watching him with love, putting George far from her thoughts once and for all.

"What's the special occasion?"

"I owe you dinner, remember? You won it fair and square."

"So, you do, and you picked the perfect night." He turned toward her.

"I did. Why?" Katherine frowned, wondering if she had forgotten something.

Alistair dropped to one knee and pulled out a ring box. "I got this back from the jeweler. I had to have it resized, and it took a bit." He opened the box, and it was a lovely classic cut diamond solitaire.

"It's beautiful, Alistair!"

"Hold out your hand," he instructed as he took it from the box. "It belonged to my grandmother, Elizabeth."

"Are you sure? Shouldn't someone else in the family get it?" Katherine felt the tears as they fell down her cheeks. It was a perfect fit, and it made everything very real.

"It should by rights go to Aunt Lizzy, but since she has no one to pass it on to, she was happy for me to pass it on to you. It'll keep the Stevens name." He kissed her hand. "Tomorrow night, New Year's Eve, we will meet at the house in Kent and get married. It's all been arranged. Most of the family will be there. Only Aggie, who is due any day, and Mave, who's not up to traveling, will be absent."

"I feel bad! They both missed Christmas because of me." Katherine shook her head.

"It's the way it is in our family. Even if we aren't there in person, we're there in spirit, but if it helps we'll have them join us via video." Alistair looked at her anxiously.

"You will marry me tomorrow?" he asked.

"Yes!' she nodded. "My sisters!"

"They're already in Kent. I sent them there instead, and they're helping Mom get everything ready." He had thought of everything.

"It's a good thing you did," Katherine said, thinking of George. He'd never find them there.

"Tomorrow?" he asked.

"Tomorrow," she agreed, and he swept her up in his arms, kissing her.

This would be her life. She would always have Alistair and his entire family to call her own. It was more than she could have ever wished for in a single lifetime.

The End